A THRILLING SAGA  S0-BUY-934

FILLED WITH ADVENTURE, ROMANCE,
SUSPENSE, VIOLENCE

IN THE GRAND MANNER OF KIPLING
AND CONRAD

❀   ❀   ❀

# THE LAST
# RUN SOUTH

## Robin Hiscock

A BERKLEY MEDALLION BOOK
published by
THE BERKLEY PUBLISHING CORPORATION

To Jack, Nate, Al
and F.M.S., if they ever read it;
and Pete,
who will.

Published by arrangement with
Alfred A. Knopf, Inc.

BERKLEY EDITION, JULY, 1960

BERKLEY MEDALLION BOOKS are published by
The Berkley Publishing Corporation
101 Fifth Avenue, New York 3, New York

Printed in the United States of America

THE ROAD to the waterfront led out of the square and
up a long hill. For about half-way there were shingle-
wood stores on both sides. Nobody was up yet, and the
blinds were still drawn on the windows. The road was
lined with bare trees, and ice lay around the roots and in
the crevices of the sidewalk like broken glass. Farther up
there were houses, the painted wood frames cracked by
the weather that came in from the sea. Gravel had been
scattered around on the sidewalk to give foothold, but
every now and then the sailor's feet skidded, and once he
came down on one knee.

It was a typical small seaport town, and the sailor
thought, as he climbed, how he had been in many of
these, making that same walk down to the front. Sometimes early morning, like now; other times it had been
just after the street-lamps had been turned on in the
evenings. Yes, especially that time, he thought. But
never before as cold as this.

When he came to the crest of the hill he paused, holding the grip, looking down to the valley in front. He felt
the full force of the icy wind coming in up the estuary,
cutting over this hill, then down across the flat country
behind him. And there now, below him, were the river,
the jetty with its single warehouse, and tied up alongside, looking quiet and toy-like from this height, the
ship.

The sailor followed the river with his eyes, seeing how

5

it curved, gradually widened, finally passing out to sea between two low headlands crowned with trees. He looked to see where it was, exactly, that the grey of the river joined the clear blue fringe of the deep water. But it was too far, and now the pale orange of the winter sun was dazzling on the small waves as it rose between the headlands. He waited there, prolonging this moment that he had been looking forward to for so long.

It had been over two years since he had last sailed in a ship; two years of working ashore after the big strike that had broken the Canadian seamen's union and nearly all their shipping fleets with it; and though he had often thought of this moment of return to the sea during that time ashore, it was without really believing that it would come about. Now here he was, and down there was the ship; he felt he was coming home.

Just before the bridge a dirt road turned off to the jetty. The stern of the ship stuck out past the warehouse. As he walked along this road the sailor could see somebody on board emptying a can of rubbish into a big drum. The man looked up from what he was doing, watched the sailor for a moment, then disappeared out of view. He was wearing a white jacket. Probably the cook, the sailor thought, suddenly feeling very hungry.

When he came round the corner of the warehouse nobody was in sight. Picking his way over the broken slats on the jetty, he tried to read the name of the ship on the stern. The white letters were faded and indistinct, and the sailor could only read the first two letters on this side. $V \ldots A \ldots$ something. Ropes of rust hung from the outlet holes in the side-plates. Hasn't been dry-docked for years, the sailor thought. It looks like a real death-ship. The Panamanian flag clung limply to its pole on the stern. I'll bet they fit her with wheels if there's no water. Or maybe the crew turns to and drags her out. She was a rough old girl, all right. But, looking at the ship, his chest was suddenly very full and he felt twice as tall.

The derricks were topped as they had been left by the dockers from yesterday's loading, and when the sailor got to the top of the gangway he saw the hatches were still open, the big wooden covers piled up against

6

the coamings. The sailor hesitated a moment, then put down his grip by the gangway and walked along the deck to midships, where he figured the galley must be. He smelt frying and heard the clatter of a lid.

"Hello there," he said, standing in the galley door.

The cook looked up from the pan of eggs. "You want something to eat?"

"Sure. I'm the new A.B."

"That's what I think when I see you. So I come back and cook some more eggs." The cook picked up a rag and opened the oven door. "Here—you eat yours now. The others are still asleep."

He pulled out a plate with some bacon on it, scooped four eggs out of the pan, and gave it to the sailor.

"On this ship we eat good. Even if we don't have a pot to spit in, we eat good," the cook said gravely.

The coat he was wearing was about four sizes too large for him. The cuffs were turned back in a thick roll over his wrists, and the shoulder seams hung half-way down his skinny arms. His thick black hair was heavily greased, and his eyes were very big and dark.

The sailor grinned. "Where is everybody?" he asked.

"Everybody is still in their lousy bunks."

"Don't they even post a watchman on this ship when she's in port?"

"I am the watchman. I keep the lookout from my bunk."

The sailor laughed. "How many are there in the crew, anyway?"

"Six on deck. Six below."

"That's all? Just enough for the watches?"

"That's right. Is a cheapskate company. The pay is no good, and the ship will go down any minute, I think. Last trip we had bad weather. I lay in my bunk waiting for the goddam bottom to fall out. The only thing is we eat good. And that is because the Mate is a pig." The cook spoke good English. Just the trace of an accent.

"My God, I'm going to love this ship," the sailor said, grinning.

There were steps outside coming up from the deck. A small boy stood in the doorway. He looked like a young relative of the cook's. He had the same thick black hair

7

and dark eyes. He was wearing a violent-looking two-tone gabardine jacket and a flaring yellow shirt. He looked as if he could use another eight hours' sleep.

"Hey, you, Johnny-Boy, you dozy bastard—where you been? You want these eggs to be like rubber? Come on —take them back to the messroom," the cook shouted.

Yellow Shirt shrugged his shoulders and started putting the breakfast into a metal container.

"Johnny-Boy will show you your bunk," the cook said to the sailor. "When you come back I expect the Old Man will be up."

The sailor followed Yellow Shirt back along the deck.

"You have to carry the food like that every meal?" he asked.

"Yes. This ship too old. No goddam good," the boy said. "Last trip I get nearly washed away three times."

They climbed up the ladder on to the poopdeck and went inside down the companionway to the crew's quarters.

It was quite dark inside the cabin. At low tide the jetty was above the level of the porthole. A chipped metal frame supported the two bunks. There were a mirror, a small table, and clothes strewn over the bench under the porthole.

"Hey, you—Svensson—you want your eggs today?" Yellow Shirt shouted, punching and poking at the mass of huddled blankets on the top bunk.

No answer.

The sailor tossed his grip on to the thin mattress covering the lower bunk.

"Hey, you—Svensson—you still drunk? Goddam you!"

Yellow Shirt got a handful of blanket and started dragging. Suddenly a huge paw whipped out from underneath and clipped the boy on the side of his head.

"Shut up, you noisy Greek scum," said a thick voice.

"You goddam-no-good-square-head," shouted Yellow Shirt. He put his hand up to his ear, standing well back from the upper bunk. He went out then, and the sailor could hear him going round to the other cabins, shouting and bawling, trying to wake the crew.

When he came back the sailor was unpacking his gear,

8

stowing it away in one of the drawers under the cupboard.

"Everybody sick," he said simply.

The sailor grinned. He finished unpacking, pushed the empty grip under the bunk, and sat down.

All around him now he could hear the sounds of the crew getting up, coughing, mumbling, stamping their feet. Right now he was still a stranger. But in a few hours' time, when the ship was at sea, when he had stood his first watch, he would be secure, confident, where he belonged.

After a while he got up, took the letter from the company out of his leather jacket, and went out on deck. The tide had turned, and already the floor was inching up over the shingle. The ship, which was resting on its keel, would soon be afloat.

Yellow Shirt was sitting outside the galley peeling potatoes. He said he would show the sailor where the Old Man's cabin was. They went up a companion-way to the officers' quarters, which were below the bridge.

The sailor knocked twice on the varnished door.

"Komm in."

The Old Man was leaning over the wash-basin, drying his face in a towel. His blue serge pants were tied round his waist with a pair of red braces. A thick woollen vest, buttoned down the front, covered his arms to the elbows.

"Signing on, sir," the sailor said.

The Old Man dropped the towel and reached for the envelope in the sailor's hand. He poked a forefinger under the flap, tore it open. Holding the letter at a slant to catch the light, bushy white eyebrows frowning, he read it slowly, turning it over to stare at the back of the sheet when he had finished.

"All right," he said at last. "Have you a seaman's book?"

The sailor fumbled at his hip pocket, taking out the small blue book, and gave it to the Old Man.

"Have you had your breakfast yet?"

"Yessir."

"Good. Then you will sign this, please." The Old Man unlocked the thick square ledger which lay in the middle of his desk. Holding open the pages with an old, heavily veined hand, he watched the sailor sign on.

"That is all, Collins," the Old Man said. "The Second Mate will be on deck now, I think." Then, as Collins turned to go, he added simply: "I hope you will like this ship." Collins looked at the Captain, slightly embarrassed, and nodded.

After the sailor had gone, the Old Man picked up the seaman's book. He studied the date on the last entry. Two years ago almost to the day. The Old Man grunted. The sailor was nearly caught that time, he thought.

He sat there at the desk, the book hanging in his outstretched hand now, wondering how it must feel to be a sailor and on the beach for so long. He, the Old Man, the Captain of this and many other ships before, had not been ashore for longer than—he didn't think it amounted to more than one year in fifty. His leave he never took unless forced to. Even then it had never been more than a fortnight at a time. Except for once.

And, thinking of that time, he got up, reaching for his jacket and cap hanging behind the door.

After the rest of the crew had finished breakfast they started covering the hatches and lowering the derricks ready for sea.

Collins and the other A.B., Svensson, a stocky, barrel-chested Norwegian, tossed the heavy wood hatch covers up off the deck to two dark Greek seamen, who slid them in place along the cross beams.

The hatch covers were of the old pattern; as thick and heavy as railway sleepers. The tops of the hatches were about four feet from the deck. As they started on the last hatch, bending for the first cover, Svensson said: "My God, I think I die." His eyes were glazed, and last night's beer was soaking out through his clothes.

"I'm bushed myself," Collins panted.

His belly and arms ached with the lift and swing. He had forgotten how rough this could be if you weren't used to it. But really enjoying it. He was falling back into the old routine of the ship and the sea.

When the mid-morning coffee came, Svensson filled

two mugs and brought them over to where Collins was sitting.

"A-h-h—this is what I wait for all morning," he said as he sat down. He took off his knitted cap and stuffed it inside his shirt. "We have a big night last night," he added cheerfully.

Collins grinned. "You been in this ship long?" he asked.

"It is nearly one year now."

"Been on the same run all that time?"

"Yes. Like a ferry-boat. Up and down. We load up here, then go south. Sometimes we go to different places, but always it is north and south."

"Where do we go down south?"

"Most times Bienvida and then Ferragas. One time, two or three trips ago, we were at Tampico. Sometimes to Matanzas—you have been to Matanzas?"

"Yes. A long time ago."

"Ah, that is a wonderful place. But everything is very expensive."

"What's Bienvida like?"

"Is a small town. Not many ships call there."

"And the other place—whad'ya call it?"

"Ferragas. That is near Bienvida. There we always load the sugar to come back."

As they sat talking, the pilot came up the gangway. They were ready to sail. Collins went along forward to the fo'c's'le-head. There was a knocking-banging sound in the steam pipes that ran alongside the hatches from the engine-room to the winches. As they went up the fore-deck Collins could see the Mate bending over the big valve that let steam into the windlass.

The Mate looked round from screwing the valve as the crew came up the ladder. Collins nodded to him as he passed by, and the Mate just went on unscrewing the steam valve. Collins turned round once as he passed over to the far rail, and the Mate was still watching him, chewing on a cheap black cigar as he laboured at the valve. After a moment the Mate stood up, a thick-bodied man with very short legs, went over to the rail, and shouted down to someone on the jetty. Then he turned and pointed to the offshore line. The crew began to unwind the heavy rope off the bitts; and all the time they worked Collins was aware of the Mate's small eyes still on him, his peak cap down low over his swarthy stubbled face, drawing hard on his cigar.

Almost imperceptibly the ship began to yawn away from the jetty. The bows inched past the end of the warehouse. From the fo'c's'le-head they could look down on to the flat roof: an empty paint-can, a torn jacket, last year's rubbish in the guttering. The ship shook as her stern bruised a fender against the jetty. It was the last contact. Collins felt as excited as if it were his first trip.

When the crew came out on deck that afternoon after dinner, the land was a low edge, far astern.

# 2

THAT NIGHT COLLINS had the first trick at the wheel on the twelve-to-four watch. The sea was calm, and the ship held easily to the course.

The wheelhouse was in darkness. The compass light, enclosed in the brass hood of the binnacle, glowed softly over the floating circle. The Mate was in the chart-room at the back of the wheelhouse. The acrid smell of his cheap cigar and the click of dividers were the only distractions in the black night.

Just before two bells the Mate came out of the chart-room. The smoke of his cigar rolled back from the glass as he peered out into the night.

"What are you steering?" he asked. His voice came out in a strangled rasp. Like he's been kicked in the throat, Collins thought.

"One-seven-one degrees, sir."

"You signed on today?"

"Yessir."

"Then why didn't you report to me?"

"I saw the Captain. Then when I came down the Second was ready to throw on the hatches."

"You should have come and seen me."

Collins didn't say anything. The Mate went back into the chart-room and Collins could hear him unrolling more maps. What's he picking on me for? Collins thought uneasily. The stupid bastard saw me on the fo'c's'le-head this morning.

A few minutes later the Mate was back in the wheel-house.

"What are you steering?"

"One-seven-one degrees still, sir."

The Mate stood in front of the binnacle and opened the little spy-door to check the course. The compass card hung easily, the degree mark opposite the thin line painted inside the cover.

"Keep a good course. We shall be in the shipping-lanes soon."

Collins stood on the grating behind the wheel, hands apart on the spokes.

"Did you hear what I said?"

"Yessir, I'm on course. Have been all the time."

"I will not take insolence. Do you hear me?" the Mate almost shouted.

At two bells the Greek seaman came up to the wheel. Collins told him the course, then stepped into the chart-room to repeat it to the Mate.

The Mate looked up from the charts. Collins noticed the trembling hands, the small eyes stuck above fat, stubbly cheeks.

"Keep a sharp lookout for other ships."

What does he take me for—a kid on his first trip? Collins thought as he walked up to the fo'c's'le-head. The Mate's attitude had taken him on the raw. The ship had been on course—what the hell was the matter with him, anyway? Maybe he's always jumpy at night, he thought. He looked pretty shaky, like he'd been drinking heavy. Maybe that's it. He'll probably be all right tomorrow. I'll have to be careful, though, Collins thought. I've got to hold this one down. Apart from the Mate, it seemed a pretty good berth. And it was good to be back at sea again, feeling the heavy dip and lift of the deck, good to be back after those two long years ashore.

He had spent nearly half his life at sea. He had first shipped out as a mess-boy when he was sixteen, and

13

from then on he had sailed out of nearly all the big ports.

Then came the strike that landed him and thousands of other Canadian seamen on the beach. He had hung around the shipping-offices in Vancouver for a while, but there were no berths. And any kind of work was scarce now. The chances of getting a berth in one of the foreign ships at the big ports was very small. It took capital to be able to hang around waiting for the odd chance, and if you didn't have capital you were through, because the ports were full of seamen. Some, a very few, squeezed into the American union. But that took even more capital.

About a year ago, when he had been working in a restaurant, he had moved in with a waitress who was on the same shift. He had left the job soon afterwards, but he had gone on staying with the waitress.

Her name was Anne. She was thirty-five, two years older than he.

Three days ago he had met a seaman he had been shipmates with some years back. It was he who had told Collins about the little company down on the Atlantic seaboard who sometimes signed on sailors who weren't in the American union. So he had heard.

When Anne came home from the restaurant in the afternoon he was sitting in the chair by the window, ready to go. She had taken the news quite calmly. She couldn't understand really why he should want to go. What had he ever got out of going to sea? She knew that he didn't like working ashore, but he had quite a good job and she had a little money put aside. They could get married, she said.

But when she saw it was hopeless, that his mind was quite set, she gave up arguing. Well, he could go and try to get a ship. If there was nothing doing, he could always come back.

She would wait for him.

She was there, waiting for him, along with the job he never liked, the stuffy room, the possibility of marriage. He was on the plank and they were waiting underneath, ready for him when he fell.

Next day, during the time they were working on deck,

14

the watches were put to scraping and chipping the paint from the midships bulkhead.

From time to time the Mate leaned over the bridge rail to see how everything was going. And when he did, a wedge of black ash would crumble from his cigar and fall on to the hatch below. He didn't say a word to Collins the whole watch. And Collins thought he must have cooled off—got used to his face or whatever it was that had bothered him.

The Second Mate came down to the mess-room while they were having tea and asked Collins and Svensson to go around the ship checking that all doors were closed and everything movable was lashed down. They were expecting bad weather.

Collins and Svensson did the rounds, checking the wedges that battened down the hatches, lashing down an empty drum that was falling about in the centre-castle. The ship was beginning to roll. It was Svensson who found the paint-locker door unfastened. There were two lockers, one on either side of the ship, that went under the fo'c's'le-head. The paint-locker was on the port side. The Mate had the key, and he had forgotten to lock it earlier in the day.

"I bet that's the first time the Mate forgets to lock this up," Svensson said.

The lock was an automatic one, and before snapping it shut Svensson held back the door and they looked inside. Cans of paint were stacked around on the shelves and piled up on the deck.

"Jesus—he must be going to paint the whole ship," Collins said.

Svensson swore. "This is the first time I get a look in this locker since I been on board."

"How do you get paint when you want it, then?"

"The Mate he always mixes it and gives it out. He don't allow anybody to come in here."

"Well, there's enough to paint a fleet in there."

Then they closed the door, snapped the lock, and went aft to report everything secure and shipshape.

That night when Collins went up to take the wheel the ship was rolling heavily. There was not much wind

15

yet, just a heavy swell, and the sea rushed past in a series of long, round-topped waves.

The first person Collins saw as he stepped into the wheelhouse was the Old Man. He was standing with one hand on the engine-room telegraph, tall and gaunt, peering out of the windows. His shoulders were hunched up, and his long yellow-white hair covered his coat collar.

Just as Collins took the wheel the Mate came lurching out of the chart-room on his short legs.

"What are you steering?" he asked. For once he wasn't smoking a cigar.

"One-seven-three degrees, sir."

"Bring her back—bring her back! The course is one-seven-five degrees!"

Collins pulled down on the spokes. "I only just got the wheel," he said loudly.

The Mate turned his head quickly towards where the Old Man was standing. Nothing happened. The Old Man took no notice, if he had even heard.

The Mate went back into the chart-room.

He pulls that stuff again and I'll tell him to take the wheel himself, Collins raged. He gripped the spokes tightly. Two degrees off in a sea like this and he jumps me. He recognized this anger of his, what it was. Pride at being a seaman, pride at being known as a *good* seaman. He didn't care about anything else.

When Collins rang five bells at the half-hour, the sound seemed to rouse the Old Man. He turned from the window and went and stood by the chart-room door. He leant one hand against the jamb, blinking his eyes in the light.

"We are through that now, I think," he said to the Mate inside. "I will turn in."

Collins heard the Mate say something; then he came out, following the Old Man across the wheelhouse.

As he passed in front of the binnacle the Mate paused to light a cigar. Collins felt he was being watched in the match-flare. He took no notice, head bent watching the compass card.

The Mate dropped the spent match, and Collins sensed rather than saw the sudden lunge of his hand.

The click of the spy-door in the binnacle and then,

again: "What are you steering?" came the rasping, disembodied voice.

"One-eight-one degrees, sir." The course had been altered in the night.

"I will look for myself. You have already been off course before tonight."

Twice this now, in the same watch; it was more than Collins could take. Hatred of this stupid bastard flared up instantly.

"My God, I'd just taken the wheel from the other man. How in hell could you expect me to keep it dead on course?"

The Mate must be crazy, Collins thought, utterly bewildered.

"I don't stand for this talk! I'll have you fired off this ship before you can turn round!" The Mate's voice was a tight scream now.

Collins looked down at the compass card again. Easy does it, he told himself, feeling the choking, tightening of his throat. He's off his nut, he must be mad.

The Old Man had paused, one foot each side of the water-step of the wheelhouse door. His colourless eyes looked from the Mate to Collins.

"What is the matter?" he asked, speaking to them both, it seemed to Collins.

"He has been off course tonight. When I tell him, he is insolent," the Mate said. The end of his cigar bobbed up and down as he spoke.

The Old Man stared at the Mate.

"What is the course now, then?" he asked Collins.

"One-eight-one degrees, sir."

"Is that right?" the Old Man asked the Mate, the rising Scandinavian inflection in his voice seeming to give the words a sarcastic tone.

The Mate turned as if to have another look in the spy-door. Come on, you crazy bastard, Collins thought. I've got you stopped dead this time. The ship was right on course.

But without waiting for the Mate's answer, the Old Man stepped out on to the wing of the bridge, slamming the door behind him. The Mate hesitated a moment, then stamped back to the chartroom.

At four o'clock Collins climbed down from the bridge. He felt wide awake and disgusted. He'd never been treated like this at sea before. He told himself not to take any notice of that crazy Mate. Just let him shoot off his mouth—I should worry, he thought. The Old Man was on his side, he could feel that.

The light in the galley was on. Mickey, the Australian, was there with the other fireman in his watch.

"Hello there, cobber," he said as Collins looked in the door. "How you like your new ship?"

"Seems all right."

"Christ save me from anything worse," said the Australian. Collins had spoken to him a couple of times during the day. He had close-cut dark hair and wore a filthy old vest with a sweat-rag tied round his neck. A lean, wiry man.

"Well, I can stick it. One ship's mostly as good as another to me. They'll have to throw me over the side to get me off this one."

"That Mate been trying to get a grip on you yet?"

"Whad'ya mean?"

"Take it easy. I could tell just looking at you. He tries it on all the new men."

"What's his idea?"

"Search me. He don't bother us down below. You ought to ask Svensson about him."

"What can he do if the Old Man don't back him up?"

"That's where you're wrong. Cookie told me that the Old Man got fired back in the Old Country after he was in some kind of smash-up. He's only holding on to this job by his eyelashes. One little upset and he's on the beach for good. And, believe me, that Mate knows it. He'd like that Captain's cabin."

"Well, after tonight he's going to love me, then!"

"He'll do his best to run you off the ship, if he can."

"What in hell for, though? I can do the work. What's he go throwin' his weight around for?"

"Search me. You want to act like Svensson. Take no notice."

"That's what I'll do, then, all right," Collins said. But it wasn't going to be as easy as that. How can I stick working with that crazy bastard?

18

Lying in his bunk later, he tried to work out some kind of plan. The idea of being turned off at the end of this trip, going back to Anne, finished with the sea, kept racing through his mind.

And that he could not face.

Next morning at breakfast he didn't feel so good. He had tossed and turned in his bunk, trying to work through this problem that now confronted him, until at last he heard Yellow Shirt, the mess-boy, coming down to set the breakfast.

He got out of his bunk then and dressed.

"Hello there, Big Jay," Yellow Shirt said. Big Jay was the name the mess-boy had given him after he had seen Collins's signature in the Old Man's ledger. He sat across the table, watching Collins eat.

"How long it takes to become an A.B., Big Jay?" he asked.

"Three years. But I've known guys do it in less."

"The Captain told me next time there is a job I can go on deck."

"Jesus—I wouldn't take in no lines with you at the winch."

"Hey, what you mean? I make damn good sailor."

"The hell you would! Probab'ly run the ship aground."

"Ahh. I bet you I make this ship go so straight it takes half the time to get in port," Yellow Shirt boasted.

Svensson walked in, belting up his pants. He reached out and ruffled the mess-boy's hair.

"Gottdam noisy Greek boy," he said. "Wakes everybody up in the whole ship."

"You lousy squarehead," Yellow Shirt said furiously, trying to knock Svensson's cap off. Svensson held him away with his huge hand, roaring with laughter.

"Yellow Shirt tells me he's coming to work on deck, Svensse," Collins said, grinning at the mess-boy, who stood glaring at them both.

"My God. That day I will jump overboard and drown," Svensson said.

When Yellow Shirt had gone back midships to serve the officers' breakfast, Collins said: "He's a good kid, that mess-boy."

"Ya. But he goes crazy ashore. If Mickey and I go for a drink, he is sure to find us. And everything we do he must do too," Svensson said. Then he paused, looking at Collins cautiously. "Mickey was telling me that you are having trouble with that Mate."

"Yes, that's right. I don't know what gets into him. He's just looking for trouble."

"He has tried that with me too. But now I just laugh at him and then he doesn't know what to do."

"Well, maybe that's the best way," Collins said. And at the time it seemed the simplest plan. I can take anything, he thought, just so long as I hold this job down. And, indeed, the whole affair didn't seem so bad this morning.

After dinner Collins went round to the foredeck to see what they were working at now. He found the young Greek seaman on the earlier watch painting red lead over the area they had cleaned yesterday. It was about half done.

The Greek handed him the paint-brush and started walking away. The handle was filthy with red lead, and, looking into the tin, Collins saw there was only a thick sediment at the bottom.

"Hey, you!" he shouted after the Greek. "How's about cleaning this brush up once in a while? Haven't you got any paraffin?"

The Greek blushed and mumbled something. He spoke hardly any English.

"All right, all right. I'll get some myself." Collins started towards the paint-locker, then remembered about the Mate having the key. He went back midships.

The cabin door was ajar and Collins could see the Mate brushing his hair. He looked quite different without his cap. His hair was shining with grease, parted dead down the centre, combed back flat on either side. He was turning his head from side to side, loving himself in the mirror. When Collins knocked, the Mate jumped back a step as if he'd been goosed.

"I need some more red lead, sir. And some paraffin to clean the brush."

"What's wrong with the brush?" the Mate asked, taking

his cap off the back of a chair. He held it by the peak, casually blowing at an imaginary speck of dust.

"Well, it's all dirtied up."

"This is not a luxury liner. You will have to get used to dirtying your hands on this ship," the Mate sneered.

"Well, how about some more red lead, then?" Collins said, controlling his rising anger.

"I will get you some in a minute. But you must make it last. I cannot afford to keep giving it out in bucketfuls. We are very short of paint."

The Mate jammed his cap on his head, and Collins followed him along the fore-deck.

"You wait here. I will bring it to you," the Mate said when they were outside. "I won't have you men spilling paint all around the locker."

No paint, Collins thought. Not much. Just a couple of hundred cans of the stuff up there. I bet he makes more than twice his wages on that stuff, selling it off down south.

"You managed to find some, then, sir?" Collins said when the Mate brought the can back half full.

The Mate looked at him quickly. "What do you mean?"

"Oh, I just thought we might be all out of red lead."

"You mind your own business," the Mate said, breathing heavily. "I'm in charge of the paint-locker. You don't have to worry about what we got."

Collins let that one go. He'd get that Mate in his own time now. Although he had tried to kid himself out of thinking about how the Mate had been riding him, it stuck hard. He'd catch him one time or another.

# 3

THEY FELL IN with the land just after midnight. As Collins walked along the deck to go up to the fo'c'sle-head he could see the Mate already waiting up there and could smell his cigar in the hot offshore breeze. The Mate was standing with his hands in his pockets, short legs straddled to the ship's roll. The meaty, black-stubbled face watched Collins closely as he came up the ladder.

"What line do we want out first, sir?"

Collins stepped up close to the Mate. Something in the way the lighted cigar swivelled from side to side of the watching face half-hidded by the dark and the slant of the peak cap made Collins think the Mate was laughing at him. Suddenly he was so mad he wanted to force the issue and jump the Mate here and now. He stepped in so close the Mate himself had to step back.

"Starboard."

And Collins turned aside then. He could tell the Mate had been startled, and it gave him a savage pleasure, but as he moved over to help the rest of the crew with the lines, he knew it had been a stupid thing to do, just the sort of thing the Mate wanted. And as he bent down to lift the big line, the thought of how nearly he had played right into the Mate's hands made him cold with despair.

Later, as they were putting out the gangway, Collins saw a soldier waiting on the dock. He wore a big picture-hat like one of Napoleon's boys, and his tunic was undone down the front. A short rifle hung from a sling across his back.

"My God, what's the idea?" Collins said to Svensson. "Is that a *sword,* for Chrissakes?"

"That is the guard," Svensson said, wiping his hands on a bit of cotton waste. "The people here are very friendly, I think. They take care of you so good. And it saves having a watchman from us," he added. "So we can all go ashore and get drunk."

The soldier grinned at Collins, then went midships.

"Where's ole Gold Teeth goin' now?" Collins asked.

"To the galley for his supper. He must eat some time," Svensson said.

"You mean they trample all over the ship like this?"

"Sure. You better lock your cabin tonight, Big Jay."

For the rest of the watch it was all right for just one man to stay on deck. They weren't going to start unloading till the morning. Collins told the Greek whose watch it was that he could turn in. Collins would hang around on deck—he didn't feel like sleeping, he was still too wound up.

He went along to the galley to see how Cookie and Gold Teeth were getting along.

"Hello there, Big Jay," Cookie said, waving a ladle. "You come to join the party?"

Gold Teeth was sitting on the table that was bolted down on the other side of the stove. His boots were off, and he wore no socks on his dirty feet.

"What's that you're eatin'?" Collins asked, looking into a stew-pot. There was some kind of meat floating around in a dark gravy. The whole mess was yellow with rice.

"That is my 'Monkey Special,'" Cookie said, ladling some out on to a dish and handing it to Gold Teeth. "Want to try some, Big Jay?"

"Why not? You mean you got up just to cook this general here some supper?" Collins asked, watching Gold Teeth bolting the meat and rice.

"Sure. It's the Old Man's orders. This way we may get unloaded on time. We must show these people we are civilized."

"And what happens if we don't feed them?"

"Then all sorts of things may go wrong. The dockers may strike, the winches break down—you never can tell about these matters."

Just then Gold Teeth finished his first plateful, and Cookie got busy with the ladle again.

Gold Teeth grinned at Collins. "Hey, you—you like?" he said, jerking his head at the stew-pot.

"That's right," Collins said.

"Plenty food, then"—pointing in the direction of the town—"plenty food, then——, hey?" Gold Teeth's gesture suited the word, and he started laughing. It sounded like a cross between a child and a jackal.

"*Cigarillos?*" Gold Teeth wanted a smoke now.

"No cigarettes," Collins said, tapping his pockets to show they were empty.

Gold Teeth jumped down off the table and padded out of the galley in his bare feet.

"Where's he off to now?" Collins said.

Cookie shrugged. "You heard him. He wants a smoke."

In a few minutes Gold Teeth was back, grinning all over his cat-face. He held up three cigars in his baby fist.

"My God—the Mate's cigars!"

Collins stared at Gold Teeth for a long moment, then stepped out on to the deck. The light was on in the Mate's cabin and Collins saw his peak cap dangling on the opening-stud of the port. He thought, too, he could see the haze of cigar smoke, and immediately, as he remembered the Mate's cigars in that Indian's hand and all those paint-cans up in the locker stacked and ready to be disposed of at the Mate's pleasure, his depression rose to fury again. It was just too easy for that Mate.

He had his hand on the paint-locker door when the sound of running feet on the deck behind him made him turn suddenly around.

The Mate was bare-headed and out of breath from his short run up the deck. "What are you doing here?" he barked. "You think I give out paint in the middle of the night? You want to start work now, is that it?"

Collins waited before answering.

"Just getting some air," he said finally.

"Your watch is over. Why haven't you turned in?" The cigar smouldered between hairy fingers.

"Just getting some air," Collins repeated. Out of the side of his eye he could see Gold Teeth coming towards them.

"Maybe you think you can pull some trick—eh?" the Mate said.

"Whatd'dya mean?" Collins felt his face flush.

"What do I mean! I am asking *you* the questions."

Gold Teeth was standing by the Mate's side now, grinning at Collins.

"I think it is a good thing we have a guard on this ship," the Mate said, looking at Gold Teeth, dragging on his cigar.

"Depends what he's guarding," Collins said.

"Well, Collins, I tell you something. I think you are too big for this ship. We do not need you to see that everything is all right around here. I am the Mate, and I can manage that."

"Keep your dirty mouth off me."

"Get to your cabin! Get off the deck!" the Mate shouted hoarsely.

"I'll go in my own good time."

As Collins turned away, the Indian started laughing.

The cackle followed Collins all the way back along the deck. Going down the companionway aft, he could hardly breathe.

He undressed slowly and got into his bunk. One of the dock lights shone just outside the porthole. Behind it Collins could see the sky growing pale over the mountains. They looked almost red in the early morning. Outside a truck started up with a sudden roaring clatter, and dogs yelped from the town.

Think your way out of this one now, he thought, stretched out hard and flat on the bunk, gripping the iron bar at the back with his hands.

It's easy. All I have to do is laugh at him, like Svensson says. Take no notice when he bawls me out, don't care if he sends me down from the wheel, let him wear himself out trying to ride me. But he was not Svensson, and that was the difference.

He lay awake till morning.

When they came out on deck after breakfast the stevedores were sitting around on the dock waiting for the crew to uncover the hatches. It was still fresh and cool at this time of day. The sun was hidden behind the island in the bay, but the rays reflected and shimmered off the clear water, stabbing the eyes. Two pelicans were diving for fish.

Gold Teeth came out of the galley, buttoning his tunic, puffing another of the Mate's cigars. He came down on deck and took up his position by the gangway, every now and then leaning over the side of the ship and spitting down between the sideplates and the dock. He was putting on his best general's act for the stevedores' benefit.

As the crew went past him to the fore-deck, he looked at Collins and started his jackal's laugh. Collins stopped in front of him and stood staring at him hard. The laughter broke down in jerks like a stalling car.

On the fore-deck they started throwing off the hatch covers. When they had got about half-way on No. 1 hatch the Mate came out and stood by Collins and Svensson. He watched them working for a while, then said: "You think we have all day, Collins?"

Svensson looked at Collins, worried. They reached over together to pull a hatch cover down on to the deck.

"By God, you have to learn to work harder on this ship, Collins," the Mate said, ignoring Svensson.

"We clear them off as quick as we can," Svensson said quickly, watching Collins's face.

"*You* will," the Mate said, grinning. "But this Collins doesn't like work. He thinks he is too good for this ship. Isn't that right, Collins?"

Not this morning, Collins thought. You don't get me this morning as easy as this. As they grabbed another cover he saw the worried look still on Svensson's face. He winked to show him it was all right. He couldn't be provoked this easy. He wasn't going to let the Mate win just as he wanted, getting him mad, then having the pleasure of being able to fire him in front of the rest of the crew.

The sun was over the top of the island in the bay when they started on the second hatch. The sweat was dribbling off the crew's faces now. The Mate was still there, goading Collins, laughing at his own jokes. Did he think he would like to be Captain? Perhaps Collins was dissatisfied with his pay? It was just as well that he, the Mate, had all the ship's keys. Otherwise Collins might be tempted to sell the spare lines. Or even the paint-cans, though they had very few of these. Hardly enough for their own use. The Mate shook with laughter at the idea.

When he came close, Collins could smell the drink in his breath. He was very sure of himself now, the Mate. And he had an audience.

The crew worked in silence. Svensson didn't look at Collins any more as they worked together, lifting, heaving, lowering the covers, sweat stinging their eyes, shirts stuck to their backs, caught between the sky and the already burning deck.

But the Mate was still there, following them back to the after-deck, just dodging into his cabin for a fresh cigar and a drink once in a while. He kept pouring it on, telling him what to do. Was that the way they did things on the other ships Collins had worked in? How did he ever get to be A.B.? Gold Teeth was with him now, his head cocked to one side as if he could actually see the words coming out of the Mate's mouth. When the Mate laughed, he laughed, not understanding a word. And the hoarse rasp of the Mate and the jackal cackling of the Indian reached even up to the bridge, where the Old Man had been watching quietly.

During tea Svensson said he would go up and draw the money from the Mate. He and Collins and Mickey were going up to the town that evening.

"What's the matter, Svensse?" Collins said. "You think I'm scared to ask for my own pay or somethin'?"

"Take it easy, cobber," Mickey said. "Svensse only thought it would save time. He's gettin' mine too."

Everybody in the ship knew that the Mate had been baiting Collins all afternoon. They had all been waiting to see what was going to happen.

They were all waiting for him to break, of course. To turn and strike the Mate, do something. Particularly Yellow Shirt whose eyes followed every movement. The kid was disappointed in Collins. But nothing had happened. He had just gone on working around the deck.

Once ashore, it was very hot, and going up the road to the dock gate the dust was waist-high. The sky was a thin blue, the colour of salt-washed denim. A truck passed them, scuffling some dust over Svensson's new tan shoes.

"Dirty monkey!" he shouted after the driver.

A wire fence surrounded the dock area. When the guard had waved them through, the three seamen walked along the road into town. The low, one-storied buildings were all made of the same kind of white-grey stone. Very few of the houses had doors; instead, just a piece of hanging cloth.

On the right-hand side of the road, in the first block of buildings, was Michael's Bar. The road widened out just there, and four big American cars that were used as taxis were parked outside. The front of the building was painted in two different colours, the lower half blue, the upper half a revolting pink. There were two entrances, each with knee-to-chest-high swing doors like the ones in Western saloons in the cowboy movies. Instead of a signboard, a small anchor hung by the flukes, and across the front of the building, just below the roof, was painted

HOTEL—MICHAEL'S BAR—FOR SEAMEN

Mickey, Svensson, and Collins went inside and sat at

27

a table near one of the doors. There was just the one long room, with a bar along the back and a big juke-box jammed across one corner. As they came in, a fat old Indian woman, jelly in a pink dress, got up from behind the bar. She was Michael's wife.

"Hey, Momma," Svensson called. *"Tres cervezas. Three beers."* He held up three fingers.

"Hokey, boys."

Momma slid the top off the big deep-freeze and took out the beer-cans. When she waddled over to the table with them her feet made a slapping noise on the stone floor. The cans were freezing-cold, covered with drops of condensation.

"This is for me," Svensson said, tilting his head back. The lump in his throat worked like a piston. They drank the first can in silence. Svensson jerked his empty down on the table first, crushing it in his huge fist, wiping his mouth with the back of his other hand.

He gave a big sigh. "A-h-h-h. Hey, Momma! More beer," he called.

"Pretty good beer for a local brew—eh, cobber?" Mickey said to Collins. "Jesus, it's hot, though!"

"That juke-box working?" Collins asked when they had drunk the second beer. He felt restless, very tense.

"Sure. Give it a spin," Mickey said.

Svensson was over at the bar getting some more beer. It was early yet, and they were the only people in the place except for the taxi-drivers, who were playing cards at another table.

Collins went over to the juke-box and dropped in several coins. The neon bulbs flashed, and the big machine purred. The tune names and bands were written in English, mostly big Latin American groups like Prado, Chavez, with one or two American records. Collins pressed some numbers at random and went back to the table. The record on the turntable spun round a few times, then the needle caught and Michael's Bar jerked alive with big brass and shuffling rhythms.

"Hey, Momma! More beer!"

Later on the place began to get crowded.

Svensson was up at the bar again, roaring with laughter at something old Momma was saying. There was no wind

28

outside, and the place was full of smoke in spite of the big whirring fan in the ceiling. The juke-box was going full blast.

Somehow, though, Collins couldn't shake out of his mood. Mickey was kidding around with Yellow Shirt, who had just come in with Cookie, and Svensson kept going back to the bar for refills and everybody seemed to be having a great time. But it wasn't right; the feeling at the table was strained. Nobody could forget the business between the Mate and Collins today.

Collins got up and went out to the toilet in the back yard. Looking up over the low roof of the bar, out to sea, he saw the sky was black with clouds. A squall was blowing in. The near slope of the distant mountains was black too, but the sky was still light overhead there and the sun behind threw the peaks and ridges into sharp outline.

When he went back inside the bar Collins was conscious from the way they were sitting, somehow settling back when they saw him coming, that the rest of them had been talking about him. The thought made him angry. His first trip in two years and it had to be like this. And earlier, when Svensson had suggested riding out to the desert outside town—that is, to the big bars and hotels where the girls were—he had said no, thinking then of Anne, as if he didn't wish to be somehow unfaithful.

This angered and irritated him too. Why think of her when he had promised himself there was no going back? It was as if he had recognized that the whole thing was hopeless, and had given up.

As Collins sat down, a little man, no bigger than a jockey, wearing a white silk shirt and ski-cap, pushed through the swing doors and stood behind Svensson's chair. The big Norwegian tilted back his umpteenth can of beer, and the little man slid a hand like a snake's head round Svensson's neck and nipped his throat.

Svensson choked, spilling the beer down his shirt. He whipped round his arm and caught the little man in a head-lock. The little man gave a shrill scream like a rabbit caught by a stoat.

"Well, look what I have caught," Svensson roared. "It is the big swindler himself, by God! I have been looking for this Michael all night." He let the little man, who was the owner of the bar, go free.

Michael pulled up another chair and sat down at the table. Momma, without being told, came waddling over with a free round.

"I have just seen your Mate, Svensson," Michael said in his piping boy's voice. "He is having a good time tonight!"

"What was he doin'?" Mickey said, looking at Collins.

"He was drinking with his friends in town. Why doesn't he spend his money here?" the little man said.

"What friends has he got, then?" Collins asked, clearing his throat. It was the first time he had spoken for a long time.

"Hey, Michael, how's about lending me five thousand bucks?" Mickey called across the table, abruptly changing the subject. His flower-pattern beach shirt was stained with beer and sweat. They were all of them gassed up now.

"Lend *you* money!" Michael squeaked, waving his hands about so that his many rings caught the coloured lights from the juke-box. "I may be sailing again myself next week. Tonight up in town all I hear is talk of trouble. I think we may have a revolution here soon now. Then what will happen to me? Last time the bandits stole my taxis, broke the juke-box. Whatever side wins, it is bad for me. You know what is the first thing they do? They put a new tax on me. Every time they have a revolution I pay for it. One more and I will be broke!"

"That is true about the revolution, then?" Svensson asked.

"Sure. Already there is trouble over in the west." The little man mopped his face with a big blue silk handkerchief. "I shall be ruined this time for sure."

Svensson looked at him and started laughing. "I bet you say this every revolution—eh, Michael?" He laid a huge arm across the small back. "By God, I wish I lose money like you, Michael. Then I *know* I'm rich."

The little man got up and flapped his arms in a hopeless gesture. "I wish I had never come here," he said. Then he moved off across the room towards the bar, still mopping his face with the handkerchief.

The crowd was thinning out now, and Momma came across and latched the doors back open. Outside it was dark, and lights showed in the houses opposite. It began to rain. They sat there watching the big drops pitting the dust. In the quiet between the records they could hear dogs fighting somewhere in the distance.

Presently a taxi pulled up outside and a thickset man got out backwards. When he turned to enter the bar, Collins saw it was the Mate.

# 4

THE MATE paid off the taxi and came through the open door into the bar. He was dressed up like a Cuban pimp —spotless white ducks, hand-tailored with stitched lapels, a fifty-dollar Panama with a red-and-gold band set back on his head, and white canvas shoes with round wooden heels.

"Jesus! Look at this!" Mickey said. "It's the Queen of the Fairies!"

"Hello, boys." The Mate grinned, moving around the table opposite Collins. "Having a party?"

"Until you came along, Queenie," Mickey said, putting one hand behind his head, rolling his eyes.

"Shut up, you dirty scum," the Mate snarled. He glared at Mickey for a moment, then looked over at Collins. And the stupid grin came back on his face. He had been drinking, but not too much.

"Well, if it isn't Mr. Collins! How are you tonight, my friend? Everything is all right, I hope? Plenty of money to spend?" The Mate laughed at that one, clutching the back of Yellow Shirt's chair.

Collins held a can of beer, looking down between his knees, taking no notice. He was pretty drunk and was trying to get his head clear by focusing his eyes on a crack on the floor.

Still laughing, the Mate edged round the table and,

standing between Collins and Cookie, put his arm on Collins's shoulder.

"I don't think our friend Collins is very well tonight. We must make the most of his little stay with us. I think he will be leaving us soon—eh, Collins?" The Mate was bending over, talking in Collins's ear. Michael had come across from the bar when he had seen the Mate, and now he had hold of his elbow, was trying to drag him away.

Collins looked up from the floor and, staring hard at the white grinning face above him, said: "Take your dirty, stinking breath away from my ear."

It was the first time he had spoken to the Mate all day. And as he said it he felt his head grow clear and he was ready.

The Mate looked surprised. He had had his fun, but it was beginning to pall even for him. It had needed Collins's participation to be really effective, and Collins had been unresponsive. The Mate had been expecting Collins to break out all day. Then he could have been fired on the spot. The Mate was a careful man, and the plan had seemed foolproof. Who could have foreseen that Collins would take everything in silence? And now, looking down at Collins's grinning face, the Mate felt suddenly enraged. He realized that Collins had been laughing at him all day. And he slapped Collins's face as hard as he could with the back of his hand.

Just as he did this, the juke-box was in between records and the sound of the slap jerked everybody round in their chairs. Then another record dropped, the bar was full of the screaming brass and beat of a mambo, and everybody was left watching Collins as he wiped his hand across his bleeding lips.

Collins put his hands down flat on the table to get up, shaking his head, and the Mate knew that this was a fight. He'd gone too far.

He put his hands quickly over Collins's shoulder as he was getting up, still dazed from the slap and slow with the drink. Grabbing Collins by his shirt-front, he spun him round and stepped in close. Holding Collins like that, the Mate brought his knee up hard into Collins's groin. Collins screamed and fell back across the table with the Mate on top of him. Empty beer-cans scattered over the

32

floor. The Mate pushed Collins's head back hard on the table, moved his feet to get a better hold, and slipped on one of the cans.

Everybody was standing up now. Svensson and Michael grabbed the Mate and pulled him away. Slowly Collins got up off the table, his eyes wide open, holding himself with both hands.

"Let him go. Let me take him, Svensse," he whispered.

"My God, are you all crazy?" Michael screamed. "You want to have me lose my licence?"

"Let him go, Svensse," Mickey said. "I'll watch out for the Guards." He moved across to the doors. Nobody acted drunk any more.

The Mate's Panama had fallen off during the struggle, and he strained against Svensson and Michael, trying to get free. The juke-box had stopped, and somebody went across and fed it money, pushing down all the buttons.

When the music had started, Collins tried to say something, then just waved his hand meaning for them to let the Mate go. Svensson shrugged his shoulders, taking no notice of Michael, who was shouting at him to keep hold, and let go the Mate's arm.

The Mate turned and pushed Michael away, then came towards Collins, flat-footed, head down on his chest, watching Collins warily.

Collins lifted his hands, set himself, waiting. He stood slightly bent over. He saw the Mate looking at the floor, and knew the Mate was seeing if it was clear of cans so he could make a rush. When he came in, the Mate feinted with his left towards Collins's face, then looped round the right, aiming low. Collins blocked it with his hip, feeling the sharp stab of pain shoot up his side, hooking hard at the same time with his left to the Mate's jaw.

The Mate's head twisted as if he were trying to look over his shoulder. Then his left hand was behind Collins's neck, pulling Collins's head down to his knee.

As the Mate pulled, Collins came forward fast, not resisting, catching the Mate off balance, running him back on his heels for a few paces before they fell, Collins on top.

The sudden rushing fall and their combined weights

33

as the Mate went back underneath on the stone floor forced all the air out of the Mate's lungs in a gasping rattle.

Collins was on his feet quickly, gaining strength now every second. As he watched the Mate lying there, the hair disarranged, the face white with pain, his hate for this man, who was now slowly picking himself up off the floor, the back of his white suit filthy with dirt and spilt beer, was so much he couldn't wait. Before, he had been protecting himself. Now he wanted to kill the Mate, but not too quickly.

The Mate was stunned, and Collins, moving in, easily went under the right round-house swing, hitting the Mate fast, twice, between the eyes with the left and in the belly with a short right.

The Mate grunted, knees bending forward, arms outstretched, hands spread in front of his face. Collins hooked him again with the left as he went down, feeling the shock right down to his feet; then, following right through with his arm, bringing it up high, he smashed the point of his elbow down hard into the Mate's neck as he was falling.

The Mate rolled over once, groaning, then lay still, face down.

Collins stood over him, gasping for breath, staring down at the dirty-white back, wanting the Mate to get up again, savagely disappointed that it was all over so soon.

For a moment nobody moved. Then with a blaring crescendo of brass a record finished in the juke-box, and in the sudden awful silence that followed everybody came alive. They came crowding around Collins, looking down at the lumpy figure on the floor.

It was over.

Cookie knelt on the floor, pushing the Mate's eyelids back with his thumbs. Mickey came running over from the doors.

"My God, Big Jay—" was all he could say.

Michael staggered out from behind the bar with a bucket of water, moaning and muttering to himself.

Svensson and Mickey led Collins to a chair. He was feeling sick again now, and the pain was worse. Svensson pushed his way through a crowd of seamen to the bar.

Everybody was feeling thirsty again, talking and laughing, and Momma was stacking the beer-cans on the counter as fast as she could dig them out of the deep-freeze.

Michael kept looking around, torn between a desire to help Momma rake in the cash and at the same time get the Mate on his feet again before the Guards came.

When Svensson came back with the beer Collins was pillowing his head on the table. He felt desperately sick.

"Big Jay, I think you were goin' to kill him."

Collins turned his head in his arms and stared dully at Yellow Shirt. He looks as happy as a kid on Christmas Eve, Collins thought, making himself grin at the boy. "He'll be all right, kid. Well enough to fire me, I expect."

"How you feelin', cobber?" Mickey asked anxiously, leaning over Collins.

"Ah-h. O.K. in a minute. He couldn't touch me, could he, kid?" Collins said, still grinning fixedly at Yellow Shirt.

"You be champion of the whole world if you want," the boy said happily.

"Pass me one of those beers, Svensse," Collins said. When he had drunk it he felt better and turned round to see how the Mate was doing.

Cookie had poured the whole bucketful slowly on the Mate's face, and there was water all over the floor. But he was coming round.

"He goin' to be all right, Cookie?" Collins asked.

"Sure. I fix him up when we get back to the ship."

"How we goin' to get past the guard at the dock gate?" Mickey said.

"Michael will drive us back in his car. We can pretend we are drunk in the back seat. It will be easy."

The Mate's mouth was wide open, and he was groaning. Svensson went across and told Michael he was to drive them back. The little man waved his arms around and said he would be ruined for life, but he went outside to get the car ready. He would be glad enough to get the Mate out of the bar before the Guards heard about the fight. Luckily, none of the townspeople ever came in the place, except the taxi-drivers, and they had packed up before it happened. It was about one o'clock in the morning now.

When everything was ready Svensson and Cookie lifted the Mate under the arms and dragged him across the floor and into the back seat of the car out side. The rain had stopped, and the sky was clear. There was a clean, fresh smell in the air after the rain, and it was quite cool.

Yellow Shirt and Mickey sat in the front seat with Michael. Svensson sat in the far corner of the back seat on the side nearest where the sentry would be at the dock gate, then there was the Mate propped up between Svensson and Cookie, and in the other corner Collins. His face was not marked like the Mate's, but it looked grey.

When they got near the dock gate the three of them in the back with the Mate started singing and fooling around. The car pulled up at the sentry, and Svensson shoved the passes out of the window. Cookie was bending down, holding the Mate as if they were looking for something on the floor. Collins turned his face away, looking out the other side.

They had a bad moment when the sentry flashed his torch on to count them, and once it looked as though the sentry was going to tell them to get out so that he could search the car to see they weren't bringing any liquor back with them. But Michael said something, and after he had looked at their passes the sentry waved them on. And they were through.

Michael turned the car right alongside the ship and they all got out. Svensson and Cookie bundled the Mate up the gangway between them.

Gold Teeth was sitting on the hatch when they came up on deck. He took one look at the Mate and started jabbering away in Spanish. But they took no notice, pushing past him and going along midships to the Mate's cabin. Gold Teeth couldn't touch them now they were in the ship. He stood there with his mouth open, watching them. It was some sight.

They had passed the galley and were going along the passage when the Old Man came out of the officers' mess next to the Mate's cabin. He had his jacket and shirt off and stood there in his thick woollen vest with the red braces round his waist just as when Collins had first seen him.

The Old Man stepped aside to let them pass, not saying anything, then followed them into the Mate's cabin.

Cookie and Svensson laid the Mate out on his bunk. He was half conscious, groaning and twisting his head around on the pillow.

"Is he hurt on his body?" the Old Man asked Cookie as he loosened the Mate's collar. The Mate's face was all puffed up now.

"No. He will be all right soon," Cookie said.

"How did this happen?" the Old Man asked quietly, looking straightaway at Collins, who was sitting in the chair by the table, massaging himself with his hands.

"I had a fight with the Mate, sir," Collins said in the silence.

"Are you hurt?"

"No. I'll be O.K. in a minute, sir."

The Old Man turnned to Cookie saying: "Stay with him a while. I will be down later." Then, "Collins," he said, "I want to see you up in my cabin, now."

Collins followed the Old Man up the companionway to his quarters under the bridge. As they went in, the Old Man said: "Just a moment," and went across to the portholes to pull the curtains without switching on the lights. Before he did this, though, Collins saw the Old Man pick something up off his desk and put it behind a big double-sided photograph-holder.

"You will find the light-switch just by your elbow," the Old Man said in the now darkened cabin. "Now I want you to tell me exactly what happened.

"You know, of course, this is a very serious matter," he added as Collins sat down in the straightback chair. "Were you drunk?"

"Well, I'd been drinking, sir, but it wasn't that. The Mate started it. He slapped my face."

The Old Man grunted and brushed his hair back with a hand. He looked very tired and old standing there in his vest.

"What did the Mate slap you for?" he asked after a while. He seemed distant, bored, as if he already knew the answer.

"He's been riding me ever since I came aboard. Yes-

37

terday he followed me around on deck when we were getting the hatches off. He was trying to start something then."

Collins felt limp and exhausted. He knew everything was all over now. He stared at the photos in the holder on the desk. A big jolly-faced woman smiled rather embarrassedly, her head slightly tilted up to the lights—the photographer had done his best. Collins couldn't see the photo on the other side of the folder.

"You are fired, of course." The Old Man's voice sounded flat, still disinterested. "You will be paid off when we get back up north."

Collins felt slightly surprised at the apathy he himself felt at this moment. So he was fired. It was what he had been dreading, but now, somehow, it seemed so simple, so obvious. He had made the decision himself, sometime between when the Mate had slapped him and he had started getting up from the table.

"You understand I don't want to do this, Collins," the Old Man was saying. "But there is no other choice now. Why didn't you come to me at the start? Perhaps I could have done something then. . . ." The Old Man looked away from Collins for the first time.

He's lying, Collins thought, staring again at the photo on the desk, feeling giddy suddenly, imagining he was in that room now, staring out of the window down to the park opposite, hearing the sound of Anne's feet on the stairs as she came back from work. He's lying. He couldn't have done anything any time.

Collins jerked his eyes away from the photo, looked across the cabin. The Old Man was sitting on his bed. He seemed unaware that Collins was even in the cabin. His right hand was absent-mindedly smoothing the worn cover on the bed. He was staring at the photo on the desk.

Probably his dead wife, Collins thought, bending forward to stand up. His body was still hurting him, and he wanted more than anything else in the world to go back aft and lie down on his bunk. Once the pain had eased a little, he would sleep for hours. The Old Man was still staring at the photo.

"Is that all, sir?" Collins said, standing now.

The Old Man's colourless eyes looked up then. It was

as if they had been bleached by countless baths of salt water.

"I must go and see to the Mate presently," he said, getting up off the bed. "You will have a drink before you go, Collins?" He added: "You will find a glass by the basin there."

As Collins turned, the Old Man lifted the whisky-bottle and glass from behind the photo frame. He screwed the cap back on the bottle, then set it down openly on the desk again until Collins had fetched the other glass.

When he had half-filled the two glasses the Old Man sat down on the bed.

"You have had bad luck in this ship, Collins," he said. "But you are young still. There will be others."

"With a bad discharge?"

The Old Man shrugged. "Your discharge will be all right. That at least I can promise you. You will be better off this way, I think."

"I don't think I'll stand much chance, sir. Our union was busted two years ago. Now we got no ships, and the Yank union is watertight."

"Unions," the Old Man said gently. "Sometimes I think the unions do seamen more harm than good. At least when I was young a good man could always get a ship. Now it is all politics. Even in this country it is all politics." He got up and held out his hand for Collins's empty glass. "Tonight the agent here told me they are expecting another revolution." He looked round at Collins from the desk, holding the third-full whisky-bottle in one hand. "This will be the seventh revolution they have had since I joined this ship. Seven! And we will be here at least four more days unloading. Then if I'm late getting back north the company will want to know why. What is a revolution to them?"

Collins stood in the centre of the cabin, sipping the whisky, feeling the flush spreading all through his body. Might as well stand here and drink. I'll have plenty of time to catch up on my sleep now, he thought.

"They know nothing of the sea, or ships, or men," the Old Man was saying now, still talking about the hated company. "Everything is figures to them. Bad weather, hurricanes, revolutions . . ." For a while he stopped and they both drank in silence.

"Will you go back to your old job ashore, then?" he suddenly asked.

"I didn't have any special job," Collins said. "I took anything that came along. When I could." That was what he was going back to, he thought. Anne and no special job.

"I am sorry about all this, Collins," the Old Man said again. He sounded as if he meant it too. "But you understand it would be impossible for you to stay now. The Mate has friends in the company." There was no getting round it. It was something the Old Man had understood clearly for a long time now.

"That's all right, sir. I'll be O.K." Collins watched the Old Man curiously.

"I will write a letter for you, Collins. It may be of some help to you in getting another ship. I used to have many friends. Some of them may remember." The Old Man lifted his free arm from his side in a vague gesture.

"Thank you, sir."

Collins put down the empty glass. He was feeling slightly drunk again.

"I will not forget about the letter."

The Old Man put his hand on Collins's shoulder as they walked across to the door. He left the whisky-bottle unstoppered on the desk, as it had been befoe they came in. And they went down the companionway to the Mate's cabin.

Cookie was sitting on a chair by the bunk, squeezing cold compresses on the Mate's face.

"How is he?" The Old Man bent over the figure on the bunk. The Mate opened his eyes and stared back dully. He groaned.

"It is his throat," Cookie explained. "He cannot talk yet."

Collins watched them from the door. He felt neither pity nor hate for the Mate. Just uninterested now, very tired, a little drunk. But the whisky had eased his own pain at least.

"You can turn in now," the Old Man told Cookie. "I will stay here."

Collins followed Cookie along to the galley. The coffee-pot was steaming on the stove.

"How are you feeling, Big Jay?" Cookie asked. "You like some coffee? I was just going to take it along to the others."

"Where are they all, then?"

"They are back in the mess-room aft."

Gold Teeth was still sitting on the hatch by the gangway. His boots were off, lying on the deck under his dangling bare feet. He was always going to have trouble with those boots. He looked up as they passed, then turned his attention back to the cigarette he was rolling. He wasn't much interested in what was going on any more either.

The voices in the mess-room stopped as Collins and Cookie came down the companionway. Yellow Shirt looked excited, Mickey and Svensson anxious.

"What did the Old Man have to say, cobber?" Mickey asked as soon as Collins had sat down.

"Just that I'm fired, of course."

"That's not fair, Big Jay!" Yellow Shirt cried out. "The Mate he started it."

The other two didn't say anything. Cookie got the mugs out of the cupboard.

"You can't beat up a ships's mate and get away with it, kid," Collins said. "I was lucky they didn't run me into prison straight off."

"The Old Man he knows all about that Mate, I think," Svensson said gloomily. "But he can do nothing."

"You sure you feel O.K.?" Cookie asked.

"I'll be all right. Just aches now is all. Be all right when I lay down," Collins said. His lips felt rather swollen where the Mate had slapped him, smarting when they touched the hot mug of coffee.

"He never hit you once," Yellow Shirt bragged again. Collins noticed with surprise that the boy was nearly crying.

"I don't think I have two more fights like that left in me." Collins grinned. But he meant it all the same.

"What are you going to do when we get to Bradport, Big Jay?" Mickey asked across the table.

"What can I do? Go back, get some lousy little job.

41

What else can I do? You tell me." Feeling the bitterness now come into his mouth.

"Christ, if I only had a few bucks together, I'd pay off myself," Mickey said.

"That'll be the day," Cookie said, joking.

"Whad'dya mean? You think you got a wonderful job or something cookin' on this leaky barge?"

"Take it easy, Mickey, Cookie was only kidding. What's the matter with you?"

"Ah-h-h, I'm fed up, that's what's the matter. Riding up and down on this ferry-boat month after month."

"Then you must pay off," Svensson told him seriously. "One thing I know is you are either a seaman or you must stay ashore."

"You save your precious lectures for your grand-mother, you old squarehead. I've been going to sea as long as you have. The only mistake I made was getting married."

The Big Norwegian shrugged. "Then you can get a divorce."

For a moment Collins thought Mickey was going to hit Svensson. The Australian's face was livid. But it was difficult to stay mad at Svensson.

"If you'll just get your big butt out of my way, I'm going to turn in," Mickey said finally. Svensson stood up.

"I think that's what I'll do too," Collins said.

As he was going into his cabin Cookie touched him on the arm.

"You want any aspirin or anything, Big Jay?" he asked. Standing there in the oversize white jacket he always wore about the ship, a small man with the thick black hair and large dark eyes, he looked like a golliwog.

"No thanks, Cookie," Collins said. And then he got un-dressed and lay on his bunk listening to Svensson snore

It would soon be daylight.

Collins fidgeted around on the mattress, trying to draw himself up into the least painful position. It hurt badly now the effects of the whisky were dying away.

ALL NEXT DAY the Mate stayed in his bunk. Cookie said he was still unable to talk.

After breakfast the Second put the crew out painting the sides of the ship. He didn't say anything to Collins directly, just told Svensson to go down on the dockside with the long-handled brushes and the pots of black paint. The Second had only heard about the Mate this morning, evidently. After he had read a few pages in his big Bible every evening he generally got straight into his bunk and slept like a log. The Second minded his own business, and he wasn't going to get mixed up in this kind of incident. He was nervous this morning.

Collins went down on to the dockside with Svensson. Some of the Greeks were hanging out bosun's-chairs up on the bows. The sky was clear after the rain the night before, and while the sun was still behind the island out in the bay it was fresh and cool. There was a wide, sandy beach on this side of the island. Fishermen lived there in huts built on stilts, and Collins could see them now in their small boats spread out across the water.

Collins and Svensson walked aft along the side of the ship till they reached the point where the stern curved out of reach from the brushes. Then they started painting, working back for'ard. After Collins had done a few yards he put down his brush and sat on a bollard.

"That's all they'll get out of me today," he said. Lifting the long brush above his head had brought on the pain again. He leant forward on his knees.

"Why don't you tell the Old Man you are sick?" Svensson asked. He took cigarettes out of his pocket, lit one for Collins.

"What the hell can he do about it? There's nothing in the medicine-chest for what I got."

Collins sat smoking, waiting till it was breakfast time. Last night's apathy was gone, and he was hating the

43

Mate all over again for the position he was forced into. Hating also the Old Man and his promise of a good discharge and a letter. Some letter that would be! Who did he think would take any notice of that? All those wonderful friends were probably dead and buried years ago.

And even if they weren't, was it likely that they would remember that broken-down old Captain? Enough to want to help a seaman who had been mysteriously paid off after one voyage? He should have told the Old Man to stick his goddam letter. He threw the half-smoked cigarette into the black pitch of oily scum below his feet and went back up the gangway, leaving his brush lying by the bollard. The hell with it! Why should he care any more?

On deck again he paused, looked over the side. Svensson was working farther for'ard now. He looked down at the brush. Better pick it up, he thought. One of these monkeys would only knock it off and make some beer money. Habits were hard to break even now. He went down on to the dockside again.

Yellow Shirt was laying out the breakfast things when he went back aft after putting the brush away.

"How you feel, Big Jay?" he asked as Collins sat down, resting his legs along the bench.

"Pretty good today. You got a head after all that beer you drank last night, kid?"

"What do you mean? I didn't have much."

Collins grinned. He could see the boy was pleased to think that he could hold his liquor like a real old sea-dog.

"That was nothing," the boy continued, getting the mugs down from the cupboard. "Sometimes I have had twice as much as that."

"You want to go easy, then, Yellow Shirt. You'll never get to be an A.B. if you're stupid drunk every time the ship docks."

"What about you and Svensse and the others, then? You have drinks all the time."

"Ah, but that's different, kid. I never used to touch the stuff when I was your age. I always stayed on board when we were in port and practised my splices."

The boy looked at Collins quickly, not sure if he was kidding or not. But Collins was looking out of the porthole

44

now, watching some big birds arching high above the town. He was thinking about his first trip. That had been down south too. He remembered the first time they docked and how he had been fascinated by the vultures or hawks or whatever they were sitting on the tin roof of a ware-house. There had been alligators in the river too, and some of the crew had got a big meathook from the galley and baited it with scraps and hung it over the stern. They hadn't caught an alligator, but Collins still remembered the excitement when they pulled in a barracuda—and its vicious thrashing, snapping, before it had been beaten dead.

Yellow Shirt had finished in the mess-room, and he paused by the door before he went back to the galley, trying to think of  something to say. He wanted to talk about last night, the fight; but he knew Collins didn't want to talk about that any more. He had understood it when Collins had kidded him about drinking.

"How long we goin' to be unloading, Big Jay?"

But Collins didn't seem to hear. So Yellow Shirt went back to the galley, past Gold Teeth's relief guard, who did nothing all day but sleep in the shade of the bul-wark by the gangway.

After breakfast Collins lay down on his bunk, and in spite of the growing heat he fell asleep almost im-mediately. He woke with the afternoon sun shining through the porthole into his face. The crew were coming along the deck overhead, and Collins could hear Svensson roaring with laughter as they came down the companion-way to the mess-room. He sat up on the bunk. The air in the cabin was stifling, and his head ached. Svensson was still laughing at something, and Collins could hear the muffled voices coming through the bulkhead from the mess-room next door.

Presently he heard Yellow Shirt come down the com-panionway carrying the food tins. As he got to the mess-room Collins heard Svensson laughing again. They must be kidding old Yellow Shirt about something, he thought. The boy's voice sounded very excited.

Collins got down off the bunk and started collecting his gear to go up for a shower and shave. He didn't feel very hungry. As he opened the cabin door he heard the voices in the mess-room grow louder. Yellow Shirt was yelling at Svensson now. Something about the guard.

"What's all the noise about?" Collins asked, looking into the mess-room. "Can't a fellow get any sleep?"

The big Norwegian was shaking with laughter. His huge arms and face were spattered with black from the ship's side where he had been painting all day. Yellow Shirt was looking furious. He was trembling all over.

"I kill that goddam guard!" he said.

"What's the matter?" Collins asked him.

Yellow Shirt just glowered at the towel draped over Collins's arm.

"I kill him!" he repeated.

"You should have seen it, Big Jay," Svensson interrupted. "He is coming along the deck past where the guard was sleeping when he drops the slops bucket. It was empty, and it crashes on the deck right by that goddam monkey's head. My God, what a noise! That guard was so scared he thought it was another revolution. One second he was lying down and the next he is standing up trying to pull out his big sword." Svensson started laughing again. "My God, I think Yellow Shirt wish he never came to sea then. He was so scared of that guard he nearly jumped down the hold."

"Who's scared?" Yellow Shirt shouted. "You think I scared of that stupid monkey? You lousy goddam square-head, I not scared of you either."

Svensson's big head in the knitted cap was leaning back against the bulkhead, his round good-natured face grinning up at Yellow Shirt. Collins saw the boy lean forward across the table suddenly, and before Collins could grab him from behind he had lashed out at Svensson, hitting him on the cheek-bone. It was not a very hard blow because he had to lean so far forward.

Collins slammed the now white-faced boy back against the cupboard.

"Whad'dya think you're doin', you crazy bastard?" he said, feeling the boy go limp under his hands. "You all right, Svensse?" he said, turning. "He didn't mean nothing."

Svensson had half risen, touching the place where he

had been hit with his fingers. He looked surprised rather than angry.

Yellow Shirt was huddled up against the cupboard, trembling violently. He looked as if he was going to burst into tears.

"Jesus! That was a crazy thing to do, kid," Collins said, letting him go. "What did you want to take it out of Svensse for? He was only kidding. Isn't that right, Svensse?"

"Sure." Svensson was watching the boy curiously. He had sat down again. Slowly the grin spread back over his face again. "My God, that Yellow Shirt he has a terrific punch."

Collins looked quickly at Yellow Shirt. It was going to be all right now.

"If he hadn't slipped, you'd be on the deck now, Svensse," Collins lied seriously. "Where d'you learn to hit like that, kid?"

"I'm sorry," Yellow Shirt mumbled, still looking at his feet.

"That's nothing," Svensson said, helping himself to the food, "but that was some punch." He shook his head a couple of times as if he had been badly clipped in a fight.

"You throw punches like that and the first thing you know you'll put your hand out," Collins said.

Yellow Shirt looked at Svensson timidly. The big Norwegian grinned back, his mouth full of food.

"You goin' ashore tonight, Big Jay?" the boy asked.

"Sure. Why not?" Collins grinned. And he went up to get his shower.

After tea he and Mickey sat on the fantail smoking, waiting for Svensse, who had taken some time scrubbing the black off his face and arms with paraffin.

Mickey looked very sharp in new dark-blue slacks and the gold-and-red beach shirt. He was cleaning his nails with a pocket file.

"What do you say to a ride in the desert tonight, Big Jay?" he asked.

Collins shrugged. "Suits me. Just to look, anyway."

Mickey grinned. "You'll think different when you get out there and see the talent."

"They're all whores, aren't they?"

47

"That's right. What you got against them?"

"Nothing special. One's much the same as another."

When Svensson was ready they walked along the deck to the gangway. Gold Teeth had just relieved his mate and was getting ready for another comfortable night with his boots off.

"Hey, one cigarette?" he said as they passed, putting on his most winning smile.

"*Gracias*," he said when Collins tossed him one. "You go—" he made a piston motion with his forearm— "*muchachas?*" And he sat there cackling with laughter at their backs as they went down on to the dockside.

One of the ships was just pulling out, and they stood watching for a while. It was something all three of them had seen and done themselves many times before. But it remained a fascination. They watched the lines being taken in on the windlasses, heard the mates shouting, saw the captain out on the bridge. She was a German freighter from Hamburg. Now there was only one ship besides their own tied up here. And she would be sailing the next day.

When they had watched the ship go out of the channel by the island, her grey stern shining in the sun, the green-painted pilot-boat bobbing up and down in the wake, they turned away and walked up the road past the sentry at the gate to Michael's Bar. The sun was cut in half by the mountain range now, and the buildings had long, narrow shadows. In the bar the electric fan was whirring in the ceiling, stirring the coloured fingers of paper that hung from the light-shades. Michael was sitting at a table talking in Spanish to the taxi-drivers. He got up when he saw them and came across to where they were sitting at the table by the door. Svensson slapped him on the shoulder as he passed up to the counter to get some beers. The little man winced.

"How is the Mate?" he asked anxiously, sitting down.

"Don't you worry about that Mate," Mickey said. "We come up here for a little relaxation."

"How is he?" Michael said to Collins, ignoring Mickey.

"He'll get over it. I have."

"But the Captain—what did he say?"

"Nothing—just fired me."

48

"Trouble! Everywhere it is trouble these last few days," Michael said, glad of a fresh audience. "I think I shall pack up and leave this place. I shall be ruined!"

"What is the matter with you, old swindler?" Svensson said, putting the cans down on the table. "Every time I have been here you have been saying the same thing."

"Ah—it is all right for you to talk." Michael twisted a ring on his finger and looked at Collins as if to exclude the other two who were so unsympathetic. "What will become of me if they take my business away?"

"Is that likely to happen?" Collins asked.

Michael flung himself back in his chair, spreading his arms in what he thought was a piteous gesture.

"How can I stop them?" he shrilled. "This time they will take everything. I know it!"

"Don't take it to heart so, cobber." Mickey grinned. "Just slip me a couple of those sparklers on your mitt and I'll personally assassinate all your enemies."

"Well, what exactly is goin' to happen, then?" Collins asked. "Who is all this trouble between, I mean?"

"The same as always. It is the Government and the Army. First the Army puts the Government in, then when it thinks the Government is getting too powerful the Army says it is corrupt. So there is a revolution and then there is another Government. And so it goes on—in, out, in, out. . . ." Michael pushed a couple of beer-cans around on the table as he spoke, showing exactly how it was between the Government and the Army.

"Well, one thing, it must be over pretty quick. I mean, how can the Government stand out long against the Army?"

Michael shook his head. "You don't understand. You see, the Army is not so big here. And the Government has the Guards."

"You mean those boys down at the docks?"

"Yes, of course. To make the revolution the Army must first tell the people how they are being cheated. But the Government controls the radio stations. So the Army has to start back in the *llanos*—the plains, that is, behind the mountains—where the people do not know what is actually happening." Michael was leaning forward now, speaking slowly as if to a child, punctuating each point

49

with a chopper-like cut of his hand. "Then when they have those people behind them they must first capture the radio stations so that the people in the town will *know* they are being cheated. Everybody believes the radio, so it *must* be true. But this time the Government is stronger than ever before. My God, there will be fighting —fighting—and I shall be ruined!" The little man clapped his hands to his forehead, groaning. "The people from over there—" waving vaguely towards the now darkened range—"they are all butchers and murderers!"

"There's good on you, Michael," Mickey said. "You're such a poor pitiful son-of-a-bitch I'll do you a favour. You can have my seaman's book and I'll run this bar for you while the revolution's on. I bet I could make a potful of money out of that. Enough to buy a taxi and go back to Aussie first class and have something left when I get there."

"By God, I like a chance at that too!" Svensson roared, slapping his knee hard enough to break a steer's neck.

"Yes! It is very funny, very funny," Michael said dramatically. "But maybe you will think it is not so funny when you see it!"

"How do you mean, 'see it'? We'll be out at sea by the time the cowboys and Indains get round to fighting it out," Mickey laughed. "And when we get down here again you'll still be here talkin' about the next one."

"Ha, you think so, eh?" The little man was so excited the sweat was popping out on his forehead, running down his nose. "How you going to unload your ship in time—tell me that!"

"Well, we only got three more days here at the most." Mickey and Svensson had stopped laughing now.

"Three days, you say. Well, I'll tell *you* something now." Michael glanced round the room furtively. The taxi-drivers were playing cards, Momma was sprawled out in the big chair behind the bar. "Already there is fighting in the west. Tomorrow, the day after, they will be here."

"Well, in that case," Mickey said, "you won't be havin your taxis much longer, so how about giving us a free ride out to the desert tonight?"

"Desert? What do you want to go out there for?"

50

Michael was asking Collins, still ignoring the other two. "Why go all that way out there? Is there something *wrong* with my bar? Out there you will be bitten to death by mosquitoes!" Michael seemed to have forgotten all about the revolution now. Collins tried to keep his face serious as he looked at the injured act that Michael was putting on. The other two were laughing outright. They had seen this many times before.

". . . and I am not sure the dirver will want to go that far tonight," the little man was saying, fanning himself with the long peak of his ski-cap. "Why don't you boys stay here quietly this evening?" he begged Collins. He hated to lose customers to the "desert."

"Come off it, Michael," Mickey interrupted. "You'll make almost as much off us on the taxi-ride as you would if we stayed here all night drinking your beer. And besides—" winking at Collins—"what happens if the Mate comes ashore again this evening?"

Michael got up in disgust and went to the room behind the bar. He shut the door behind him.

Svensson hired one of the drivers to take them out. The man seemed pleased to be out of the card game, and he went round the corner to get his taxi while Svensson bought an armful of beer-cans from Momma. She was still wearing the same dirty pink dress, Collins noticed. Momma counted out Svensson's change, brushing back coarse Indian hair with her brown shrivelled hand. She looked almost twice as old as Michael, Collins thought. Though he had probably married her when she was sixteen or something. Women aged quickly down here.

The taxi was a big American sedan, three years old— a little dented in the back and around the wheels, but still looking pretty trim for all that. Svensson and Mickey got in the back, while Collins sat up front with the driver. He was looking forward to the drive. He always got a kick out of seeing these different places, going along in a car. The sleep today had refreshed him, and the pain had subsided into a dull ache. And, moving along the street now, going easily over the surfaced road up into the town, past the open-fronted shops and small houses, he was trying to forget the dream he had had this afternoon just before he woke up.

51

He had been walking up the stairs to their room. He remembered them vividly. Eighteen in the first flight, then the squeaky boards just outside the bath-room on the lower landing, the three doors on the left, up the last flight of sixteen stairs to the single room under the roof. Anne had opened the door, smiling of course. "Perhaps it's all for the best," she had said. "Perhaps it's all for the best. Perhaps it's all for the best. . . ." Over and over again, like a stuck record. And the terrifying, smug smile.

"Perhaps it's all for the best." Echoing in his head, as the taxi came out into the main square. The driver turned and they went past the treelined centre, with the lights shining on the dark heart-shaped leaves, the women squatting on the paving with their baskets of fruit and stalls of food. The cafés and bars were full of people, and the taxi seemed to break through the barriers of noise that roared out into the street from the juke-boxes.

"Who's that?" Collins asked, pointing at the statue in the middle of the square. The horse was rearing up, and the man on its back was holding a sword in both hands, kissing the hilt.

"I don't know. Some old cobber," Mickey said. "Here, try one of these."

He handed over two cans of beer, one for the driver. Collins offered the man a cigarette. The driver took them both with a grunt, holding them in one hand as he turned out of the square.

They passed the last street-light and the taxi began to go faster. The radio was on, and they sat drinking the beer, listening to the faint pounding music from the car radio and watching the country. The sun had gone behind the mountains, and as they watched they saw the near slopes turn a deep dark-wine colour. Collins realized now that the mountains were farther off than he had thought coming in that night in the ship.

About a half-mile from the town the road joined up with the main coast road. They went left here. It was a wide three-lane highway, with the open desert on both sides. It was getting dark, and the big cacti, stumpy and solid, looked like pieces of modern sculpture. The headlights were on, and the pool of light drifted along the road

52

in front of them. Collins looked at the speedometer and saw they were doing fifty. The cooling air cut round his elbow resting on the open window. Several times they passed herds of goats tethered alongside the road, and once an old man muffled up in a coloured blanket rode past leading a string of donkeys.

"How far out is this place, anyway?" Collins asked after a while.

"We got another town to go through yet," Mickey said, cutting open some more beer-cans on the back seat. "And then some more."

The taxi was climbing now, and, looking behind, Collins could see the lights of Bienvida and out on the water some more lights. That must be from those fishermen's huts on the island, he thought. Darkness was dropping quickly. As the taxi levelled out along the slight gradient Collins could no longer see the mountains properly. They seemed to merge with the desert in a sloping blackness. An animal screamed out in the night.

"I wouldn't want to be stranded out there," Collins said, taking a mouthful of beer.

Svensson leaned forward to lob an empty can out the window. The suction caught it, and they heard it fall away behind them.

They saw the lights of the town over to the right a long time before they got there. They turned off the highway, and here the road was no more than a cart-track. The driver went at a reckless speed, bumping and lurching over the ruts and hollows. The town was nothing like Bienvida. Just rows of squalid-looking huts lit by candles. Hens flew out of their way, and pigs ran wild along the street. They passed only one café, and that was closing. The man turned from putting up the shutters to watch the taxi as they lurched by.

On the far side of the town the track was even narrower, and it seemed to Collins the driver was going more by instinct and good luck than anything else.

And then suddenly, as they came round the last block of huts, Collins saw that the sky was lit up in a blaze of colour way out over the desert. It looked like a four-alarm fire.

"There you are, Big Jay," Mickey said from the back

53

seat. "We'll be alongside in a few minutes."

Collins was holding on to the seat with both hands now as they bounced and banged over the track. Bushes whipped at the fenders, smacking up against the windows.

"My God, you'd think they'd build up the roads out here," he said.

"Who worries about that when you've got this far? And you'll never notice it goin' back, cobber. Take my word."

# 6

THE TAXI stopped finally on the stamped-down earth drive-up at the end of the track. It looks like a fairground, Collins thought, staring out at the neon-lit buildings. The earth drive-up was almost as long as the town square in Bienvida. Three big buildings faced them close together, and another, less garishly lit one was a little farther off to one side. There were more cars and taxis parked along the front than Collins had seen in the whole of Bienvida. And the noise. The three main bars were packed with a shouting, yelling, swaying tide of people, and above it all the never-stopping, blaring, stomping of the juke-boxes.

"How do we get back?" Collins asked as they paid off the driver.

"He'll stick around most likely until we go back," Mickey said, shoving the handful of paper change into his pocket. "And if he doesn't there's always another taxi somewhere around."

They crossed over to the raised board-walk that ran along in front of the buildings. The long, wide fronts, supported by pillars, were entirely open, no doors of any kind.

"We'll start here and work our way along," Mickey said as they approached the nearest bar.

Collins looked up at the neon bulbs strung across the top of the building. They spelled the words NUEVO

54

MUNDO, with a smaller line underneath—GRAN OTEL—all done in different colours.

They went in between the pillars. The big front part was roofed over, filled with tables and chairs. At the back Collins could see a patio open to the sky. A double-sided bar ran almost the full length of the rear of the front room, serving both here and the patio. Some place, all right, Collins thought. Big business in the middle of the goddam desert.

They elbowed their way through the crowd to the patio. A big woman with auburn-tinted hair flung her arms round Svensson, chewing at his ear as he half carried, half pushed her in front of him clearing a passage like a cow-catcher on an engine. It wasn't so crowded out in the patio, and they sat down at an empty table which had some kind of shrub stuck in a painted wood box in the middle.

"Clear that off for a start," Mickey said, putting it underneath by their feet. He turned round to look for a waiter. The woman had seated herself on Svensson's lap and was doing all kinds of crazy things, making Svensson roar with laughter.

Nothing much here for me, Collins thought. He had enjoyed the ride, but somehow he couldn't snap out of that bad feeling. He looked down at his feet. The floor was paved with small multi-coloured tiles, laid out in intricate patterns. A high-class whore-house, he thought. Full of sights and sounds. But he was bored.

Both sides of the patio had covered passages, supported by more pillars, reminding him of a church somehow. Rows of small cabins were ranged down there, each exactly similar. The door of one opposite him was open; two girls were sitting on the bed talking. A cheap-looking crucifix above the pillow, a chair, a dressing-table, and a picture of some bull-fighter tacked up on the back wall were the only furnishings. The long, sad face of the matador, sleepy-eyed, hands clutching the top of the *barrera,* stared out across some invisible ring waiting for some invisible bull.

A young boy staggered across the patio with a tray, bringing bottles of Coke and rum in cardboard cartons. As he bent over to put them on the table Collins looked at his fair hair and olive skin. He was wishing now he had never come. But it had seemed like a good idea at the time. Before, he had always enjoyed working the spots in these places.

Svensson was still playing around with the woman on his lap, and Mickey was talking to a little dark kid at the next table. He turned round, said: "Hey, Big Jay, this Sheila says she's got a friend would like to meet you."

"I'll bet she has." Collins grinned, shaking his head.

"Ah, come on," Svensson said, peering round the woman's neck. "You get fixed up, Big Jay. Then we can stay here all night."

"Don't rush me," Collins said. "You two go ahead. I think I'll mosey round and see if I can see anyone I know first."

Mickey started to say something, then shrugged and turned back to the other table again. Svensson was grinning at the woman on his lap. His eyes were slits, and his cheeks were flushed as though they had been slapped.

Collins got up and walked down to the far end of the patio where the toilet was. A big man with sandy hair was sitting on the floor holding his head in his hands.

"Mah Gawd, mah Gawd," he was saying to himself.

The back of the patio was a plain wall with a little wrought-iron gate in one corner. Collins stood for a while, staring out over the desert towards the mountains. There were no stars tonight, and he couldn't see anything farther than a few yards away. He fumbled around at the door, trying to open it. It was locked somehow, but he could not see where. There was a pattern on the top of the gate, but it was impossible to make out what it was in this light.

Mickey and Svensson had gone off with the girls when he got back to the table, so he wandered through to the front room. The smoke was thick in here, wouldn't disperse in spite of the open front and ceiling fans. Collins stood outside on the board-walk, looking up to the sky, wondering if it was going to rain.

A group of drunks staggered out of the bar behind him, and Collins stepped down on to the earth to give them room. In the next bar everything was the same— front room, patio, juke-box, girls, noise. He walked

56

around, trying to see if there was anyone here he had sailed with.

He was looking for somebody who could bridge that two-year gap when he had been ashore, somebody he could talk to about the old times—an outsider who could reassure him that he had done the right thing, taken the only way possible. For his confidence was draining away now, leaving a thick sediment of doubt.

But there was nobody there he knew, and he went outside again and sat down on a white-painted boulder that marked the perimeter of the drive-up. Three Guards were standing talking to some taxi-drivers. They turned to watch him. Collins lit a cigarette to steady himself, wondering how long Mickey and Svensson were going to be. Better take a long look, he thought. Be the last time you see this kind of thing again. He wished he could find somebody he knew to talk to, though. The noise and seeing all those boys having a good time made him jumpy.

Out of the corner of his eye he saw one of the Guards walking over to him. The Guard stopped a few feet away.

"Hey, you."

The Guard jerked his arm towards the bars, meaning that Collins should go back inside.

Collins sat still for a moment, then got up slowly and walked past the Guard, still not looking at him. One of the taxi-drivers said something in Spanish, and all of them laughed. Herd you around like bloody sheep, Collins thought furiously. Scared in case you don't spend all your money. The whole bunch of them are probably pimps. He went back into the Nuevo Mundo. Mickey and Svensson were sitting at the table again with the two girls.

"Where you been, Big Jay?" Mickey asked as Collins sat down.

"Just walkin' around."

"Get yourself fixed up yet?"

"What's it to you? You on the pimp or something?"

"Hey, what's got into you? I didn't mean nothing."

"Here, have a drink," Svensson cut in. "Then you feel better."

Collins drank a double shot of rum straight off.

"What's in that other place up the line?" he asked after a while.

"It's too expensive there," Svensson said.

"What do you wanna go there for?" Mickey said. "Isn't this place good enough for you?"

"I didn't say that, did I?" Collins said irritably.

"They probably wouldn't let us in, anyway," Mickey said.

"Why the hell not? They won't take our money, you mean?"

"Aw, listen, Big Jay. There's nothing up there special."

"You been there?"

"No. Now, come off it, cobber! What's the matter with you tonight?"

"Nothing's the matter. I just want to go and look the place over. You two can stay here. I'm not askin' you to come."

"But why waste good money?" Mickey pleaded.

"Well, I'm goin', anyway," Collins said stubbornly. He didn't really give a damn about the place. But the mean, raging feeling was almost a taste in his mouth now. He hoped those stupid Guards would try and stop him. He stood up.

"Come on, Mickey," Svensson said quickly. "We go and have one drink with Big Jay, then we come back here."

"Well, all right, then. But it's a cryin' waste of money."

"Listen," Collins said savagely, "I'll pay for the round. You won't be losing anything."

"Okay, okay. But take it easy, will you?" Mickey looked at Svensson worriedly. They got up and followed Collins across the patio.

They walked along to the end of the boardwalk and then across to the other bar. This one was set a little way back from the front three, at the far end of the drive-up. Big American cars were parked outside. The front was enclosed, with double doors in the middle. One of the doors was ajar; Collins pushed it open and they went inside.

The front room was much the same as in the other bars, only smaller, quieter. The tables all had cloths. Some people at a table turned to stare. Two of the men

58

were Guards officers. In their tight-fitting olive-green uniforms, with epaulettes, high boots, and spurs, they looked as though they were waiting to go onstage in some opera.

"What the hell they think they're looking at?" Collins said loudly, staring back. The officers looked away.

"For Chrissakes," Mickey said, "let's go out back and have this drink, then."

Collins led the way. Their footsteps sounded very loud on the stone floor. The Negro barman looked up from polishing the counter as they passed.

A big tree grew in the centre of the patio. Its branches were twined with coloured lights like a Christmas tree. A thin half-caste with a yellow face came out from the shadows as they sat down. Svensson and Mickey sat forward nervously on their chairs. Svensson put a big hand on the tablecloth, then snatched it away quickly.

The half-caste looked at them expectantly.

*"Traigame tres rons y colas,"* Collins said.

"I didn't know you spoke that stuff," Mickey said when the waiter had gone.

"That's about all I know." Collins was looking at some girls who were sitting at a long table on the other side of the tree. There was nobody else out here. The girls were eating. They didn't appear to have even noticed the three men. The half-caste walked over to the bar and started talking to the Negro. Collins saw the Negro look over to where they were sitting, then reach down and bring up a bottle from under the bar.

"Well, you might as well enjoy yourself now you're here," Collins said.

"This is where all the big-money boys come," Mickey said, looking around. "Look at those Sheilas havin' their scoff. Hand-picked, every one of them!"

"My God—you see that one in the blouse, Big Jay?" Svensson whispered.

"See her! That's not a blouse, you old squarehead! More like a fishing-net!" Mickey laughed. They were both feeling easier now.

"How much you think it cost here, Big Jay?" Svensson asked.

"More'n you could dig up."

The half-caste came back across the patio, moving silently in his canvas shoes. When he had put the drinks on the table he stood, tray under his arm, staring over their heads. Collins took a bundle of small paper money out of his pocket and started peeling them off.

"My God—that's half as much again as it costs down the line," Mickey said.

Collins shrugged. "So what? At least this place is quiet."

"The hell with that. These Sheilas aren't goin' to take any notice of us."

"Sure they will. Ask them over for a drink. Go on."

"You think they'd sit with us? You seen the kind of cars outside."

"That's nothing. If you got the money, these broads don't care what else you've got."

"I like to try that one in the fish-net all right," Svensson said seriously.

Mickey started laughing. "You can't faze that ole squarehead," he said to Collins.

Collins grinned. "Go on, Svensse. Ask her over."

Svensson stood up slowly, wiping his hands on his handkerchief. He grinned at the two of them sitting there, then they watched him as he walked round the tree towards the table where the girls were sitting, looking very truculent with his head sunk into his enormous shoulders.

"This I have to see," Mickey said, leaning forward.

The half-caste waiter was leaning with his back against the bar. He and the Negro barman were both watching Svensson now.

The girls had stopped talking as Svensson came near, and the only sounds were of cutlery on the plates as they ate. The girl in the blouse was sitting on the far side of the table. Her plate was empty in front of her. Collins and Mickey saw Svensson go round the table and start talking to her. The girl didn't look up, just sat half-turned in her chair as when she had been talking to the other girls. After a while Svensson came back.

"What she say, Svensse?" Mickey asked.

"She said she was eating her supper and she was too busy to come over."

"Too busy!" Mickey said. "There, what did I tell you,

60

Big Jay? Come on, let's go back to the other place."

"You two go on," Collins said. "I'm goin' back to the ship after I finish this drink."

"Aren't you goin' to stay the night?" Mickey asked. He looked worried.

"No. You two go on. I don't feel so good tonight somehow. I'll see you back on board tomorrow."

"You got enough for the taxi?" Svensson asked.

"Sure. In fact, I got more than I need. Here, take some."

"No. No. We're all right," Mickey said. "You won't change your mind?"

Collins smiled. "No. I don't feel up to it somehow. You two go ahead."

"Well. See you back there, then, Big Jay," Mickey said.

"Okay. Take it easy."

Collins watched them go out towards the front. Mickey said something to Svensson, and they both stopped at the bar. They spoke to the Negro for a moment, then Mickey turned and waved and they were gone.

The half-caste came across with another drink. They must have paid for it, Collins thought. He sat with the glass in his hand, staring at the tablecloth. It wasn't only the job, the ships—even the people were different, he thought. For two years he had missed the seamen he had known, even more than the sea itself. That was something he had never even tried to explain to Anne. Anne. "Perhaps it's all for the best." That would be just the kind of thing she would say, he thought. The girls at the table were laughing at something now.

Stupid sluts, Collins thought, raging. Who does that old bag in the blouse think she is, anyway?

A girl got up from the table behind the tree somewhere where he couldn't see her and walked across the patio. He heard the hard, bright tap of her heels before he saw her. She came from behind the tree and crossed diagonally in front of Collins's table. She walked almost defiantly, it seemed to Collins, striking the stone floor hard with the heels of her white shoes, her head turned away from him as she lifted the very black hair off her neck with one hand.

Collins half rose from the table, saying: *"Perdone,*

61

*señora . . ."* She stopped then, turned, still with one hand at her hair, small, very poised.

*"Que . . . ?"* she said.

"Er . . . *Quiere usted una . . ."* Collins tried to remember what the word for drink was in Spanish, then, aware of the two men at the bar watching, said quickly: "Would you like a drink?"

She paused for a moment, hands at her side now, looking at him. She shrugged. "All right," she said.

You speak English, then?" Collins said foolishly, moving a chair for her.

She sat down. "Of course." She crossed her legs, sitting slightly sideways to the table, resting one arm on the cloth. Collins looked round for the waiter. He was already coming across the patio with a tray.

"Cigarette?" Collins asked while the waiter was putting down the drinks. She slipped one out of the pack easily with her slim brown fingers. She looks like a nurse in that plain white dress, Collins thought, leaning forward to light the cigarette. Snotty bitch.

"What's that you're drinking?" Collins asked. Her hair looked almost dark-blue in this light. She was pushing it back off her neck again, taking sips of the thick green stuff in her glass. "Créme de menthe," she said. "You have never seen it before?" She glanced over Collins's shoulder. Hadn't looked at him directly since she sat down.

"I've seen it before," Collins said, losing his temper. "All you whores drink that stuff. I was trying to make conversation, that's all." She was looking at him now, all right.

"Where are your friends?" she asked. She crushed the cigarette in the ash-tray.

"They left. They didn't like it here."

"Yes? And I think it is better that you should go too."

She didn't stand up, though. She seemed to be staring right through Collins. It irritated him.

"Why? What's the matter?"

She picked up her glass again. "Nothing. You can drink here if you wish. If you have the money."

"Oh, so that's what's troublin' you, is it!" He pulled out the notes, held them out in his hand. He felt disgusted

62

with himself almost immediately. She never even looked. He put his hand back in his pocket, crumpling the money in a tight wad. He waited for her to say something, to sneer at him or laugh. But she just sat there, still slightly turned away, feeling her hair at the back. She was very beautiful. Collins was silent, watching her, trying to think of something to say that would reach her, interest her— even hurt her. Anything was better than this icy detachment.

"What do you keep doing that for?"

She looked at him, her lips slightly apart, enquiringly.

"I mean your hair. Why do you keep feeling it?"

"Oh." She smiled then. "I washed it this afternoon." She took her hand away.

"Well, it wouldn't take that long to dry in this climate," Collins said. "Would you like another drink?" he asked quickly, hopefully.

"No. Thank you. But you have one."

"I'm sorry I was rude just now," Collins said. "I don't know why I said it." He smiled nervously. His face felt hot and stiff.

"It was nothing," she said simply. "Are you from a ship?"

"Yes. I never came here before. Tell me—where did you learn to speak English?"

"All the girls here speak English. I learned at the convent. When I was at school. We had an English Mother." Well, a convent, for Chrissakes, Collins thought. She said everything so clearly, so logically. He wondered how she came to be here.

"Is it always as quiet as this?" Collins said. The girls were still at the table, the waiter was talking to the Negro at the bar.

"There are some people here now," she said. She ran the ball of her thumb round the inside of her single-strand pearl necklace. The skin in the hollows of her neck looked satin-smooth, a warm brown. "It is mostly business-men who come here. You will see them later, if you stay," she said. It seemed to Collins that she was laughing at him then, though her face was still grave, composed. Her lips were full, but not thick like those of

63

most Indian women. Her skin was no darker than a summer tan.

"Do you live here all the time?" Collins asked. He had suddenly felt very excited when she said that about staying. "I mean, you must get tired of this place."

"I go home for a few days every month. Don't you get tired of being on the ship?"

"Well, no, that's different. I mean . . ." He felt strangely embarrassed by this girl. He felt a fool for having asked such a goddam silly question. He hadn't been thinking what he was saying.

The girl laughed. It was a lonely sound in that quiet place. "Don't you know that this is work too? You work in your ship, I work here. They are equally the same." She was honestly amused.

"Yes, I know that really. I've said a lot of stupid things tonight, haven't I?"

"Yes." She smiled at him, sitting square to the table now, looking at him, not through him any longer. "But at least you are not drunk."

"Don't tell me you're bothered by drunks in this place. I thought this was strictly high-class."

"High-class? What is that?"

"Well, I mean, I thought this place was for the . . . the . . ." He paused, trying to think of a word to put it clearly, then, looking up from the cloth on the table, he saw she was smiling again. "You know what I mean," Collins said happily.

"You are very sad for yourself tonight, I think—no? You try to make an argument all the time."

"Ah-h—I don't know," Collins said, grinning, resting his elbow on the table, holding his head on his hand. "I wasn't feeling so good this evening when I came in here. I'm sorry. I mean it."

She shook her head very gently. "It is nothing," she said. "Sometimes it is the same with me." She picked up the cigarette pack, turning it over in her fingers.

"Would you like me to bring you some of those?" Collins asked.

She shoook her head. "No. There is no need for you to do that. We get plenty given us."

64

"Yes. I suppose you would." Collins felt hurt. It was senseless, he knew, but he couldn't help it.

The girl stretched over and touched his arm. "You must not be silly," she said. "Why should I tell you to bring cigarettes when I already have plenty?"

Then, abruptly, she asked: "Would you like to come with me?"

"Why not?" Collins said, trying to match his mood to hers, to appear at ease. But his hands were cold and he felt very nervous as he stood up and followed her past the table where the other girls were, to her room, which was at the far end of the patio.

She walked just slightly in front of him, her head no higher than his chest, seemingly unconcerned by the loud noise of her heels and the sudden silence at the table as they passed.

Collins stood inside her room, looking at the neat bed with the blue cloth quilt spread tightly over the top, waiting while she closed the door behind her. He could hear them talking at the table again now. The girl slid past him in the narrow space, not touching him, and Collins smelt the faint smell of some perfume. He fumbled with the buttons of his shirt.

"Put your clothes on the chair." The girl was sitting on the edge of the bed at the far end, leaning over to take off her shoes. Her hair had fallen forward, hiding her face. She undressed quickly, and as she stood hanging up her dress Collins came behind her, kissing her where the hair touched her shoulder. She turned and came into his arms.

Afterwards, lying there sleepily, listening to the voices outside, the tension gone now, Collins asked: "Can I see you tomorrow?"

"Of course," she said. "How could I stop you?"

He lifted himself up then, looking down at her, with the black hair spread over the washed blue of the cover, the small, firm-skinned body, but she smiled and reached up to him and it was all right again.

But while they were dressing she asked suddenly, as if she had just remembered: "Do you know what the time is?"

"No," Collins said. He noticed she looked worried. "Why?"

"Someone is coming to see me tonight."

Collins said nothing, went on lacing his shoes. He didn't look at her as she opened the door, and they walked together in silence along the patio to the doors. The place was filling now and the Negro at the bar was shaking up a drink in a silver flask. They stopped by a pillar. She didn't say anything, just put out her hand as she had done earlier in the evening and touched Collins's arm.

He watched her as she walked back across the patio. He didn't even know her name yet. But there would be plenty of time for that tomorrow evening, he thought.

# 7

GOING BACK in the taxi was as Mickey had said it would be—Collins never noticed the bumps. It was cold at this hour and they drove very fast along the deserted highway. The square at Bienvida was empty, the women with the stalls had gone, and the cafés were shuttered. The mounted statue looked grey in the street-lights.

It wasn't till they were turning out of the square into the road that ran down to the docks that Collins remembered he had told Yellow Shirt he would see him at Michael's Bar that evening. But it didn't worry him—perhaps the boy would be still there with Cookie. It couldn't be so very late, Collins thought. He would tell the driver to stop at the bar. He would walk the short distance to the docks.

And so, as they came round a slight bend in the road and he saw the anchor sign and the lights still on in the bar, it was with no presentiment of any kind that he turned to the driver to tell him to pull up. And he was also unprepared for the driver's sudden exclamation and the lurching, hard-braking stop that threw him forward against the windscreen. Collins's first thought was that something had crossed just in front of them. But the road was empty. The driver had cut the headlights, and several seconds passed before Collins noticed the figure that had just come out of Michael's Bar.

Sitting there in the sudden silence, except for the steady insect-hum all around, Collins and the driver watched the man stagger to the curb and sit down. The doors of the bar swung behind him twice more, then were still. The man was a Guard, and he sat there on the curb, not looking round, holding his head in his hands. He didn't appear to have noticed the taxi yet.

Collins opened the door of the taxi gently. The metal handle felt slippery under his hand. The driver did not try to stop him, just sat staring at the figure sitting on the curb. Then the bar doors were pushed outward and Collins saw two more Guards coming out, holding Yellow Shirt's legs, dragging him face down.

Collins started running then, thinking: My God, they've killed him. The boy's hands trailed very limply. Moving very fast, keeping in the shadows, Collins saw the two Guards drop Yellow Shirt's legs and stand over the other Guard. They had their backs to Collins now. He was almost up to them when his foot twisted in a rut and he went down in a hard, jarring fall. He was up on his knees almost immediately, gasping, winded. The Guards had turned round now, staring. For a moment nobody moved. Then as Collins stood up, his hands and the side of his face grazed and stinging, the Guard who had been sitting holding his head got up off the curb and came towards him. He moved with slow, jerky steps, like a man who has been badly shocked. His mouth was open and he was trembling violently. Tugging with both hands at the holster which had slipped behind him, the Guard pulled out the big black revolver. The hammer, as he cocked it, made a sharp, final sound.

Still standing there, motionless, sweat running down his back and sides, Collins felt enormous.

The Guard had been both hurt and badly frightened. He was hatless, blood was trickling down from the side of his head, and his flat Indian face was twisted into a yellow-grey mask. He stood just in front of Collins, not looking at his face, but staring straight at Collins's chest, on a level with his own eyes. His mouth was still work-

67

ing; he seemed to have lost all control over his facial muscles.

Suddenly the Guard jerked up the revolver, holding it in both hands. The fore-sight ripped up Collins's breast-bone, tearing his shirt open and leaving a thin red weal. Collins didn't move, just looked down at the burning mark. He could tell that the Guard was coming out of his shock and was working himself up to shoot.

Behind him now, Collins was suddenly conscious of the sound of a truck coming towards them from the town. He didn't dare turn his head to look. The two other Guards heard it also, because they came across and one of them put his arms around the shoulders of the wounded Guard who was still standing in front of Collins and turned him around and led him away. The Guard went quite quietly, his back shaking, breathing noisily through his mouth. The truck passed Collins and drew up outside the bar. The wounded Guard was helped into the cab, then the other two picked up Yellow Shirt and dumped him over the tail-board. They paused, looking at Collins. Then one of them said something and climbed on to the back of the truck, holding on to the iron frame above his head. The other Guard got into the cab with the driver and the wounded one. The truck turned in the road and started back into the town. As it passed Collins the truck slowed down, and, still without moving his head, Collins saw a figure lean out of the near window. But the shot never came. Instead he felt a foul, stinging jet of tobacco-smelling spittle splatter down his cheek. Somebody laughed then, and the truck picked up speed towards the town.

When he could no longer hear the noise of the engine Collins turned round. His neck felt terribly stiff. The dark shape of the taxi was still there, but he could not see the driver. There were voices in the bar now, and he started to walk towards the doors. He nearly fell at the first step, and when he reached the doors he had to make a conscious effort to lift his arm. The grazes on his face and hands, and the weal on his chest—he didn't notice them. Only this terrible aching rigidity that extended all over his body.

Inside the bar a group of seamen were huddled round

68

the silent juke-box. A chair lay on its side just by the doors. Nothing else was disturbed. Collins noticed that the fireman in Mickey's watch was in the silent group. They had stopped talking when he came in.

"Wha' happéned?" Collins said. Nobody seemed to hear. Then he realized that although he had moved his lips no sound had come out.

There was the clatter of a chair being pushed aside and Collins turned to see Michael running towards him from the counter. The little man looked terrified. There was something comical-looking about him, though. He was not wearing the ski-cap, and Collins noticed for the first time how very white his bald head was compared to the brown face.

He tried to laugh then, couldn't, put his hand up to his face, and felt the sticky filth on his cheek.

"What happened?" His voice sounded hollow. He blinked, feeling the eyelids almost stretch with the effort. Then he sat down quickly.

"It was terrible—terrible!" Michael twitched and quivered like a puppet. "What will happen to me now? My God. I ha—"

Collins reached up suddenly and grabbed him. "Not to you, you stinkin' rat-bait. What happened to that kid, that Yellow Shirt?" he shouted at the terrified face a few inches from his own. "What happened, for Chrissakes?"

Still holding Michael, he looked round for Cookie, but Cookie wasn't there. "Where's Cookie tonight? Was Cookie here with the boy?"

"I was trying to tell you," Michael sobbed. "He hit the Guard with a chair."

"Who? The boy did?"

"Yes, yes! My God, I thought they would kill him."

"He was drunk," the fireman said, coming up behind Michael. "The mess-boy was drunk. He hit the Guard with the chair. The other two came in and beat him with the guns."

Collins let Michael go then, sagging back in the chair. The white faces looking down at him made him feel sick. The shock of the scare he had had outside was only just wearing off. He had been expecting to get shot out there all the time. He could think of nothing but the slow-motion image of the wounded Guard walking towards him, the big black Army revolver shaking in his small hands.

"Give me a drink, somebody," he said, feeling for his handkerchief.

He heard the whole story from the fireman as they walked back to the ship. How Yellow Shirt had gone ashore by himself, expecting, as Collins knew, to see Collins and the others at Michael's. The fireman didn't know why Cookie hadn't gone ashore that night. I know, though, Collins thought. Because he thought I would be up there. How am I going to explain that to Cookie? After I promised Yellow Shirt. What does it matter how it happened? he thought dully, listening to the fireman explain how he and the others had gone ashore and found Yellow Shirt sitting alone in the bar, drunk, this Guard hanging round, jeering at him about something; how after they, the other seamen, had got there and had been drinking their first beer, Yellow Shirt had suddenly jumped up and hit the Guard with the chair as he was walking away; how the other two Guards, who must have been just outside, had heard the noise, come in, and pistol-whipped Yellow Shirt senseless.

"I think the boy is dead," the fireman said finally, confidently. And as he remembered the way they had dragged the body, sack-like, it seemed to Collins too that he must be dead.

But he didn't tell Cookie that when they got on board and the fireman went up to report to the Old Man, leaving Collins to push open the cabin door, stumble across to the bunk in the dark, and shake Cookie awake.

"What's the matter, Big Jay?" Cookie asked sleepily, recognizing the voice.

"Listen. Sit up, will you, Cookie? Something bad happened."

Cookie reached over to the chair where his clothes were. "Turn on the light," he said.

"No. No. It doesn't matter. You can't do anything now. Listen. Yellow Shirt got in a fight with one of the Guards up at Michael's."

Cookie slumped back in the bunk. "Where is he now? Where is he?" he whispered.

"I don't know. They took him away. You see, I—I wasn't there tonight. I forgot about saying I'd see him up there. I was out at the desert with Svensse and Mickey. I only got back in time to see them take him away."

Cookie didn't say anything for a minute. Collins could hear voices in the Old Man's cabin.

"Was he hurt, Big Jay?" Cookie sounded quite calm, resigned. His face was still hidden from Collins in the dark.

"They knocked him out, I think. He hit a Guard with a chair." Collins leant forward, moving out of the faint glow of the dock-light coming through the porthole which he felt was spot-lighting his face. "It was my fault. I forgot I told him we'd be there. My God, I'm sorry."

"No. You mustn't believe it was your fault, Big Jay. I should have gone with him myself. I stayed here tonight because I felt tired. Tired! When I knew the boy was upset because of what happened on deck today when he dropped that bucket. Did you know about that, Big Jay?"

"Yes. Now, listen, Cookie, you don't want to start blaming yourself. You couldn't know I wasn't up there."

Cookie was crying now. "But what do I tell his people? Can you tell me that? What do I say to them? And what can I say to *myself*—when I knew all the time the boy was upset? Too tired! How shall I sleep now?"

"Now, take it easy, Cookie. The Old Man will fix it in the morning," Collins said, not believing it, though. "Everybody knows Yellow Shirt was drunk. They won't do anything to a kid his age. It'll only be a fine or something."

Footsteps descended the companionway from the Old Man's cabin, and presently the door opened and the light was switched on. The Old Man stood framed in the doorway, the fireman behind him. A glass of whisky was cupped in one hand, as if he had forgotten to put it down.

He looked at Collins. "Are you hurt? Were you in this too?"

"Hurt?" He had forgotten the graze on his cheek. "Oh, no, sir, I just slipped."

"You are sure you are not in any trouble with the Guards, then?" The wrinkles radiated out like spokes round the Old Man's eyes.

"No, sir. I just saw them take the boy away."

The Old Man grunted, looked at Cookie on the bunk. "Well, there is nothing I can do tonight. I will go ashore first thing and see the agent. This is very serious, you understand." He paused, staring down at the glass in his hand, not seeming to notice it. "Well, you may as well turn in now. There is nothing I can do tonight," he repeated.

After the Old Man had gone, Collins and the fireman walked back along the deck aft.

"The boy is dead, I think," the fireman said. "I told the Captain that."

"You're probably right. We'll know right enough in the morning, anyway," Collins said.

He undressed in the empty cabin, too tired to wash, and flopped down on his bunk.

He woke from a dreamless sleep, surprised to see the Second Mate standing there instead of Yellow Shirt. Cookie carried the breakfast across that morning. He looked more shrunken even than usual in his large white jacket. He told Collins that the Old Man had already gone ashore.

"He'll probably he bringing the kid back with him," Collins said. Cookie seemed to brighten up a bit then.

While the crew were eating, Svensson and Mickey got back from the desert. Collins told them about Yellow Shirt.

"I hope they killed him," Mickey said.

"What kind of thing is that to say, for Chrissakes?" Collins said.

"What I mean is he's better off that way. If what I've heard about these jails here is true."

Svensson nodded glumly. He looked tired. "The first trip I make down here the Guards shot a Swede up in the town. There was a hole in his leg you could put your fist in. They took him to the jail. I remember because

72

next time the ship was here his friends tell me how it was at that jail. They went to see him once."

"Well, what happened to him?" Collins asked.

"I don't know. He may be still there."

"Ah, you're crazy. They can't do that nowadays. The Consul would spring him."

"Listen, cobber," Mickey said earnestly, "they had an English captain stuck up there for six months. And the Consul couldn't spring *him*."

"Well, we'll see when the Old Man gets back. My God—they wouldn't jail a kid his age!" But Collins was frightened now.

"If the worst comes to the worst, we can always go up and see him when we go to Ferragas. I think it's only about twenty miles from the jail there. That is, if they put him in that one," Mickey said.

"Well, for God's sake don't say anything like that to Cookie. I told him the Old Man would probably bring Yellow Shirt back with him."

Mickey shook his head. "I don't think Cookie really believed that. He knows what the score is down here. You see, since they started drilling oil here the crummy Indians have had it all their own way. These companies aren't goin' to upset themselves over a mess-boy." He stood up, unbuttoning his shirt. Collins noticed the beads of sweat starting at the roots of his close-cut dark hair.

"Well, there's nothing you can do, Big Jay," Mickey said quietly.

"So I keep telling myself."

"Well, take it easy. Me and Svensse are going to have a shower before we go on deck. Not that it'll do much good in this heat."

The sun had risen above the island, and already it was getting unbearably hot beneath the iron deck. It was almost as bad topside when they went up to work. There wasn't a breath of wind this morning. The sky was a pale faded blue, and the heat haze danced over the decks like smoke from a frying-pan.

The Second Mate was very worried today. The news of the coming revolution had somehow thrust itself between him and his beloved Bible. And the Captain had told him before he went ashore to set the crew working alongside the stevedores. They wanted to get the ship out of there as quickly as they could before the trouble began and they were left stranded.

All that morning Collins operated one of the winches. He wound some cloth round his neck for protection, but the sun scalded the iron winch, making it impossible to handle without gloves. The tar on the deck bubbled and pitted like a lava bed.

It was lunch-time before the Old Man got back. He looked very old and broken as he pulled himself up the gangway. His white suit was threadbare, and he carried a crumpled Panama in one hand. He stood by the hatch shaking his head before Collins said anything.

"I did what I could," he said. "But with the trouble coming it was impossible to see anyone. The agent has his instructions."

"Yes, but what about the boy? Is he alive?"

"Yes. He's alive. As far as I could find out, he was taken straight to the jail."

The heat, the nervousness of the wait, yesterday's terror, all exploded in Collins's head.

"Is that all you got to say? Is that all you found out in this time? What the hell you think you're goin' to do now —write another letter to your friends?"

The Old Man waited until he had finished. Waited till Collins had run down and stopped. Then he said, in a new, hard, cruel voice that Collins hadn't heard before: "Collins, I was going to sea before you were alive. Because you have been discharged you have no right to speak like that. Either you control yourself or get below." He paused, then continued mildly, as if nothing had gone before. "I have done all I can. I have tried every way I know. But you must understand that these people are not like us. And there is already fighting less than one hundred miles away from here."

Collins became aware that Cookie was standing at his elbow. Svensson and the others had also crowded round.

"I have warned you men several times before about how you conduct yourselves in this country." The Old Man had raised his voice now, speaking to them all. "You know their penalties are severe. I cannot be held responsible for what you may do ashore, drunk or sober."

He stopped suddenly. "I will do all I can for the boy. That I promise you," he said quietly. Then he went into his cabin.

Collins stood there looking after him. That Old Man's still got some bucko left in him yet, he thought. He felt a hand on his arm.

"You mustn't feel too badly, Big Jay," Cookie said.

Collins stared down at the deck for a moment, then walked away without speaking.

Svensson and Mickey were in his cabin. They had a bottle of some white stuff.

"Here, come and have a shot, cobber," Mickey said. He sounded a little drunk.

"What is it?" Collins asked, holding the water-thin liquid up to the light. I could certainly use a shot of something, he thought.

"That's real panthers' juice. Try it."

Collins took a big swallow. It burned like turpentine. He choked.

"That's enough of that," he said. "I want to go out to the desert tonight. I'll be needing my eyesight."

Svensson grinned. "You mean you got fixed up in that place after all, Big Jay?" He was obviously anxious not to talk about Yellow Shirt any more.

"I don't know about that," Collins said carefully. "But I'm goin' out there all the same. You two goin' again?"

Mickey shook his head. "No. Me and ole Svensse are goin' to stay here. We got two little jugs for comp'ny. It's too 'spensive out there."

"Well, you want to go easy on that stuff," Collins said. "You got the whole afternoon to do down below yet."

"Ah-h-h, hell with down below. I'm not goin' down below any more. I tell you what, cobber. I'm goin' to pay off this filthy, stinkin' ole barge next trip." Mickey snatched the bottle from Svensson. "I don't care a damn if they do fire me. I'm fed up with this lousy life. I'm goin' to wire the old woman and tell her either she comes back to Aussie with me or it's finished." He smacked his open hand on the bunk-frame. "Finished!"

"Come on, Mickey, let's go have something to eat," Collins suggested.

"No. No, I know what I'm doin'. Jus' lea' me alone."

75

Mickey stayed down in the cabin all afternoon. And when Collins went back at tea-time he was flat out, dead drunk, on Svensson's bunk. Collins changed quickly. When he came down from the shower, Svensson was pulling off Mickey's shoes.

"He's goin' to be in terrible shape when he comes out of that one," Collins said, looking down at the open-mouthed Mickey. "Did the Chief Engineer say anything, do you know?"

"No." Svensson took the shoes off gently and set them down on the deck. "He don't say anything to this Mickey. He is a good man, and the Chief don't want to lose him."

Collins had seen the Chief Engineer only a couple of times on the trip down. He was a fat, swarthy little Greek with double chins.

"Do you think he meant that about payin off, Svensse?"

"I don't know," Svensson said. "Maybe." He watched Collins change into his shore clothes. "You got enough money, Big Jay?"

"I've drawn out all I got in the ship."

"Here. I don't need this tonight. I am staying here." Svensse took out some notes and held them out to Collins, grinning. "You need all you can get, I think, if you go to see that girl in the fish-net."

"No. Not her. Another one." Collins counted over the tissue-thin notes. They looked phony, like stage money. "I'll pay you back when I get off up north," he said.

"No, I don't want it back," Svensson said. "If you pay that back, what will you use for money when you leave—buttons?" He tried to make a joke of it.

Collins didn't say anything for a moment. He was remembering the hill at Bradport when he had first seen the ship, how he had felt on that cold morning, the square with the station at the bottom. He though how he had felt he was lucky that day. The big break after two lousy years. He still could not imagine walking back down that hill, through with it all again.

He had finished dressing now, and he noticed the worried look on Svensson's face.

He shook his head. "I'm not savin' anything for the other end. Why should I care? Things couldn't be worse

76

than they are. That part will take care of itself." He felt in his pockets to see that he had cigarettes and matches. "Well, see you later, Svensse."

"Sure, take it easy with Fish-net, Big Jay," Svensson called out as Collins was going up the companionway.

The sun was still above the mountains, its lower edge touching on a ridge. The glare was full on Collins's face, making him screw up his eyes as he walked towards Michael's Bar. It had been the hottest day he could remember. The crew had gone on working alongside the stevedores all afternoon. The Old Man must be really worried about this revolution to do a thing like that. But it had certainly paid off. They should be out of there some time tomorrow night. Collins felt almost giddy with the heat. He had covered himself up as best he could at the winch, rigging a sack over his head. Two men had fainted down in the holds during the afternoon and had had to be lifted out in slings.

He wondered what Yellow Shirt was doing. Well, you can't do anything about that, he told himself. He had been worrying about it all day. Sitting at the winch, feeling the sun roast up one side of him, then directly overhead, then slowly down the other side, as though he were a lump of meat on a spit, he had gone over the whole business again and again. He couldn't seem to remember exactly what it was he had said to Yellow Shirt about seeing him at Michael's. And it had become very important to Collins that he should remember the exact words. The feeling that he had had last night, before he had met the girl —the feeling that everything was falling away under him, that he had spoilt his luck for himself, not that it had been spoilt for him by the Mate, that if he had kept his head all this would never have happened—this bad doubtful feeling had hit him a thousand times harder today after what had happened to Yellow Shirt. It was useless to tell himself to stop worrying. First it had been about his own trouble, paying the penalty for banking on something too heavily, something he had always tried to be careful not to do. And now, much worse, was the thought that he had been responsible for Yellow Shirt. It went much deeper than those words he tried so hard to remember, the words about meetin Yellow Shirt at

Michael's Bar. He felt somehow that it was his—Collins's—troubles, his fight with the Mate, the way they had laughed at the kid when he had been scared by the Guard, the whole pattern of violence—it was the sum of all these things that had been responsible for Yellow Shirt running wild with the chair.

## 8

AGAIN HE ENJOYED the ride out to the desert in the taxi—it was somehow relaxing. Also he was earlier tonight and he could see things clearer. He had the driver who had brought him back last night. Collins tried to get him into conversation, but he either couldn't or wouldn't speak English. And Collins's Spanish was limited to asking the time, the direction, or how much for the drinks.

They drove through the town and Collins was surprised to see how deserted the place was. Even the cafés were closed, with the thick steel and wood shutters up, and there were no women sitting on the sidewalk with stalls and baskets tonight. The taxi-driver didn't seem to know anything about that either. It was very quiet.

The desert itself looked different too under this light. Collins saw now that the ground wasn't the gold sand colour he had imagined but a kind of slate-grey. In between the tall cacti he could sometimes see huge stone boulders and outcrops of shingle.

They stopped once at a small filling-station on the coast highway. Watching through the windscreen, Collins saw the driver talking with the old man who appeared to run the place. A small boy was working the pump, and Collins turned round once and saw him staring sullenly through the rear window. A slight wind had started, and overhead two large black birds shifted and wheeled in the sky. Once the sun slid behind the mountains, it would turn dark very quickly.

The old man seemed to be explaining something to the driver in great detail. His high-pitched cracked old voice sounded excited, and he kept turning and pointing in the direction of a gap in the mountains. Collins wondered how the fighting was going. The last they had heard on the ship, it was over a hundred miles away. He had meant to ask Michael about it, but the little man hadn't been in the bar when he had hired the taxi.

The breeze touched his neck through the open window at his side. It came from the sea. It was going to be cooler tonight, all right.

When they turned out of the filling-station, the road stretched out ahead of them, wide, flat, and empty. The driver put his foot down and Collins watched the hands of the speedometer slowly climb the face of the dial. Forty—fifty—sixty. They levelled out at that speed, the air singing past, the big American sedan holding the road well. It was quite unlike driving through any other country Collins knew. Here you got the steady, never-changing picture of the desert flashing past you on both sides, no interruption from gradient or buildings or hedges. You could judge distance only by a slight turn in the road or an extra-large boulder. And though the coast was flat, you still couldn't see the sea from this far in.

By the time they had reached the turning that branched off into the cart-track road, only a small slice of the sun was still showing. The taxi's shadow seemed to cut through the bases of the cacti. The night was shutting in fast. The road they were bumping and crashing over now was even worse than Collins had suspected last night. Generations of old wooden-wheeled carts had gouged out deep ruts. In places the hollows were bad enough to suggest that they were originally points where the carts had got bogged down and had had to be dug out. It didn't seem to bother the driver any, though. He slowed down— a little. Collins wondered how much money Mickey must make in a year to keep a fleet of taxis going under these conditions.

As they drove through the small town at the head of the track that led down to the four bars, the driver kept his hand on the horn. Dogs came yapping and howling right up to the taxi, turning aside only just before they went under the wheels. People stood in the open door-

79

ways and watched as they drove by. There was a smell of cooking in the dusk.

In this half-light, before the neon signs were switched on, the bars looked smaller and rougher from the outside. There were only a few taxis drawn up outside, and a bunch of shoe-shine boys were playing dice on the hard earth.

Collins told the driver to stop outside the first bar, the Nuevo Mundo. He was feeling slightly nervous about seeing the girl again. He wondered whether he should go in here and have a beer first, then decided not to waste any time. If the ship was leaving tomorrow night, he'd better make the most of it now.

As he walked along to the bar at the other end where the girl was, the shoe-shine boys broke off the game and clustered round Collins, hanging on to both legs, passing the brushes lightly over his shoes as he walked. Collins noticed that most of them were half-castes of some shade or other. They stumbled and clung, fighting among themselves, all the way up to the big double doors of the bar. Then they stood round in a semi-circle, watching Collins as he turned the huge ring handle. Their small accusing faces were still there as he shut the door behind him.

There was nobody in the front room except the waiter. He was spreading clean cloths on the tables—holding the four corners of the cloth in one hand, lifting up the ash-tray and lamp with the free hand, then somehow flicking the cloth out so it slowly settled down across the table. It was a wonderful movement.

Collins ordered a beer at the bar. The Negro grinned at him today and Collins nodded his head. The girls were up at the far end of the patio, eating at the long table. Collins could not see her from here. He didn't like to walk right across to the table while they were eating. He turned to watch the waiter again. That's probably the only thing he can do well, Collins thought. He's like me. Too much pride in one small achievement. No, that's not true, he corrected himself, watching the flick and bellying of the cloths. Don't start thinking like that tonight.

He had only had a couple of swallows of his beer when he heard her footsteps as she crossed the patio behind him. He went on watching the waiter, afraid to turn round, to appear too eager, in case it wasn't her. But he knew it was, and when he heard the different sound her heels made as she stepped into the enclosed front part, he could wait no longer and he turned round.

She was smiling. "Would you like something to eat?" she asked.

"Well, I don't know, I—"

But she seemed to guess what he was thinking.

"It's all right. It is for nothing. 'For free,' " she said, teasing, using the last expression as if it were somehow amusing to her.

Collins grinned. She was wearing a different dress today, blue—very plain like the other one. He was feeling more excited at seeing her again than he had expected. Her face, when he had thought of it during the day and the ride here in the taxi, had become blurred and indistinct to him, and now, as she led him across the patio to the table, walking slightly ahead of him again, Collins tried to fix in his mind the line of her neck and shoulder, the way she held her head upright, challengingly, the fine smooth curve of her black hair, parted just slightly to one side of the centre. He studied these things carefully as they walked, trying to fix them so he would remember them as if they were the lines of a ship, the contours of a coast. And when she turned, still smiling reassuringly, she was more beautiful even than he had thought last night.

She pulled back a chair for him at one end of the table. He was conscious that the rest of the girls were watching him. When he had sat down the girl went up to the head of the table and ladled food out of a big bowl on to a plate. One of the others said something to her in Spanish, and Collins thought he heard her name. Fran-thee-ka, it sounded like. Whatever the girl said, it was something funny, because the rest of them started giggling. Maybe she's taking the rise out of me, Collins thought, wedging his knees uncomfortably under the narrow table. But when she came back and set the plate in front of him she smiled at him quite openly and honestly, and winked.

81

"You're hungry?" she asked, sitting opposite him. "You're here early tonight."

"Yes. I got away as quickly as I could," Collins mumbled.

He felt embarrassed, surrounded by all these girls who could all apparently speak English, all of them, he felt sure, listening to him now, perhaps mocking him.

"What's the matter?" she asked. "Don't you like the food?"

"Yes. It's fine." He noticed for the first time that it was a stew made with shrimps and rice. "I'm hungry too. I didn't stay to eat on the ship." He started eating quickly, nervously, not looking up. It wasn't until he had swallowed his second mouthful that he realized he was eating a hot, peppery curry.

He dropped his fork, choking, tears starting out of his eyes.

The girl threw back her head and laughed. "Ai-e-e-e. One minute he eats nothing, now he eats too much."

Somebody poured him a glass of water, and Collins drank it gratefully. He could feel the curry sliding down his gullet like liquid fire. When he had recovered himself he looked across at the girl.

She looked back at him, straight-faced. "You are all right now?" she asked solemnly. "You will eat more slowly now, I hope." And they both laughed.

When Collins had finished and she had brought two cups of black, treacly-looking coffee, he said: "You know—I don't even know your name. I heard one of the others call you something—sounded like Fran-thee-ka."

Most of the other girls had moved away from the table now, and they had this end to themselves.

"That's right." She nodded. "And what is yours?"

He told her. "But how do you spell this name of yours?" he asked.

Pointing her forefinger, she spelled it out for him on the table.

"Oh, Francesca!"

"Sí. But it is called the other way." She tilted her head to one side, teasing again. "And you—you are called Jaime?"

"Hay-may! Is that what it is in Spanish? For Chrissakes, don't start calling me that. Sounds like a fairy's name," Collins protested.

She leaned across the narrow table, so close he could smell the softness of her hair, touching his arm with her hand. "How should I call you, then, when I want you?" she said, holding his eyes with hers. She smiled slightly.

Collins knew she was only kidding around, but he felt the excitement rise in him all the same. She seemed very alive tonight. Joking with him, happy, not distant and cold as she had been at first last night.

"Did your friend come last night?" Collins asked. And in the same instant he saw that he had said the wrong thing. The smile smoothed out of her face, leaving it hard, a bright look about her eyes.

"Yes," she said distantly. She turned her head away, looking down towards the bar. The Negro was reading a paper. The coloured lights hung on the tree had been switched on some time while they had been sitting there. The place will soon be filling up, Collins thought.

"Look," he said to the girl, "I'm sorry if I said something wrong again. It's not my business." He put his hand over the slim brown wrist as it lay on the table. "Hey, you! Where have you gone now?" he said gently, desperately. He tried to joke. "You can't leave me here sitting by myself, for Chrissakes!" He lifted up the limp hand by the wrist, patting it gently on the table-top.

When she turned round Collins could see she was trying not to cry. He looked round quickly. Four girls at the other end of the table were bending over a magazine, looking at the fashion illustrations. The others had gone into their rooms.

"Now, wa-ait a minute," Collins said, bending forward, trying to see into her face as she put her other hand over her eyes. "What's the matter, Fran-thee-ka?" he whispered, using her name for the first time. "Now, I didn't say anything as bad as that, did I? Here—please don't start cryin'. If the others see you like this, they'll think it's my fault and throw me out." He pulled her wrist down over the end of the table so he could hold her hand without anyone seeing. She was still sitting there, hunched over, shading her eyes with the other hand. "And if they throw me out of here, I'll get lost in

83

that God-awful desert for sure. You wouldn't be as mean to me as that, would you?"

He felt her hand open then and hold his under the table. And she took the other hand away from her face, tilting her head back in the old way, and Collins saw happily that she was all right again. The jet-black eyes, shimmering under the moisture, where like water-smoothed pebbles.

"Ah, that's my girl," Collins said huskily. "I'm sorry to have upset you like that."

My God, he thought, she gets upset easy. I wonder why that should have thrown her like it did. He looked round to see if anybody was watching them, then pulled out his handkerchief.

"Here," he said. "Blow hard." She drew her head back, but he caught her nose in the handkerchief and, when she gave a sort of snuffle, tweaked it hard. She pushed his hand away, laughing.

"Last night it was you," she said. "Tonight it is my turn to feel bad." Collins waited, watching her across the table. "You see," she continued, "one of the girls told him that I went with you last night before he came."

"Well, who is this fellow, then?" Collins asked gently.

"Oh, he comes to me often. He doesn't like me to—" She hesitated for a moment. "He doesn't like me to see anyone on the nights when I know he is coming. You understand?"

"Who was it told him? What's it got to do with them?"

The girl twisted her fingers in his hand under the table. She shrugged. "I don't know which one. It doesn't matter. He wouldn't tell me which one. She must be jealous," she said, sitting upright now, looking down at the four girls at the other end of the table.

"Well, this friend of yours—what does he do, then?" Collins asked. He felt hurt. He didn't know why, exactly— it was none of his business, as he had said before. But it irritated him that this man should have such importance as to be able to hurt her, to come between them like this tonight.

"He is an important man," she said simply. "He is in the Army." Something about the way she said that made

Collins feel that she was more than a little proud of this "friend."

Collins let go of her hand and took out his cigarettes. "The Army, eh?" he said, watching her carefully. "Shouldn't he be up at the front now winning medals? I mean, with this revolution or whatever it is. I thought the Army was trying to throw the Government out on its ear."

"Yes. He came last night for the last time. It was very dangerous for him to come here. Everybody knows he is in the Army."

She *was* proud of him, then. Perhaps even loves him, Collins thought.

"How did he arrive—disguised as a donkey or something?" he said cruelly, feeling bitter with himself for sitting here like a dummy all evening.

"Why should you say that?" the girl asked, quite composed now, staring at Collins curiously. "He has been very good to me."

"No reason. I just thought you might be letting yourself in for more trouble when he hears I was here again tonight. And it seems to matter to you," he added coldly.

"No," she said, looking puzzled. "No, it doesn't matter who sees you here. I have shown them I don't care."

"Ah. I understand now. That's why you had me over here to eat with you this evening. So as you could prove you didn't give a damn what they or he thought or said."

She had just been using him to prove her independence. She probably hardly even saw him sitting here. Here was I, as nervy as a kitten, and all the time she was just using me, he thought. He felt disgusted with himself.

The girl was still staring at him. She looked worried now. "What are you angry about now?" she asked slowly. "Why should you worry about this?"

"Well, isn't that the truth—didn't you have me over here just to show the rest of them that you weren't worried what they thought?"

"I have just told you I don't care. I asked you here because I thought you might be hungry. What do you want me to say?"

"Just the truth," Collins said.

He wasn't sure she even heard him. It was getting

dark in the patio, and she was leaning back in her chair, arms folded. Waiting for her to reply, he had time to count the paces of a girl strolling down the patio behind him . . . four—six—eight. . . .

"It is possible that you are jealous?" the girl said, almost as if she were talking to herself.

"Jealous!" Collins laughed, trying to pretend amazement. But he was past pretending now, even to himself. Sitting there in the gloom, he had thought suddenly of Anne, the long dull evenings ahead. There had never been any flashes of pain with her, like this now. Emotion wasn't involved with Anne.

"Yes, I suppose you're right," he said, painfully aware that he was exposing himself again, not even sure how the girl would react. If she laughs, he thought, I'll get up and walk straight out of here. But she didn't say anything. Instead, she stood up, smoothing her dress, then took him by the hand and led him to her room. She shut the door behind them, switched on the light, and stood leaning back against the door, her hands behind her.

"Jealous!" She laughed softly, pulling her lips back hard over her fine white teeth.

Collins sat down on the bed, his hands between his knees, watching her. The old routine, he thought. I'll bet she's worn a patch on that door with that posture. He felt hollow and empty. For the first time he could watch her dispassionately. She was still very beautiful, whatever way you looked at her. He felt furious with himself for spoiling the evening as he had done. Like some love-sick kid. And the way he was feeling now, drained and flat, it was most certainly ruined. The violence of his emotion earlier—his fear of being made a fool of—had reached its climax and had somehow torn him apart from her. For the first time he could look at her, inspect her, as someone outside of himself.

"*Que . . . ?*" she said, puzzled by the way he was watching her. She smiled at him again. "Well?" she said, waiting.

Provocative as hell, Collins thought. They all learn it in the cradle down here. He rolled over on the bed, careful to rest his shoes over the end. Aw, hell, he thought, throwing his arms across his face, looking up at the low ceiling.

She came forward from the door, genuinely worried. "Are you ill?" she asked, sitting beside him, putting her cool hand on his head.

"Ill?" Collins echoed, grinning. He held her hand, biting at the fingers. "I'm not ill, I'm dead."

I wonder if I'll be able to share a taxi going back, he thought. He grinned again at the face suspended just above him, the hair brushed back in those dark, smooth sweeps over the small, shapely ears, the tan skin that rich women in the north could cultivate only by frequent work-outs with the sun-lamp, and the precious oval shape of the black eyes.

She looks rather sad, Collins thought.

He felt a tight, constricted feeling in his chest. She'll look sadder still, he told himself, when she finds you're going to take a rain-check this time. But it wouldn't work any more, and when he put his hands on her shoulders she fell across him without a sound, burying her face in his neck.

Collins put one arm behind her back, holding her tight, stroking her hair with the other hand. This must be routine number two, he thought, watching some insects flitting around the bulb in the ceiling. And a pretty effective one too. But when she moved her fingers across his face, touching his lips like a blind person, he felt himself give way and the words came out in a rush.

"Ah . . . you beautiful . . . ah, you lovely." He pushed his burning face against the thick softness of her hair. It was like slipping down with the fast current in a boat on a dark night. There was no going back now. She turned her face, her eyes closed, lips slightly open.

When they came apart, her eyes opened and she smiled at him. Her voice sounded husky when she spoke. "You are crazy—*muy loco,* I think."

"I'm crazy, all right," Collins said, feeling her hand like some small animal against his chest.

He looked up at the ceiling again, and for the first time she saw the graze on the side of his face. She sucked in her breath with a hissing sound, carefully tilting his head towards the light.

"It's nothing," Collins said, seeing the question in her eyes. "I just slipped, that's all." The sore place wasn't much bigger than a coin. He didn't want to go into all that now when everything was going so well. But he had forgotten about the weal, and when his shirt was finally slipped off, he sitting up on the bed, touching her face gently with his mouth all the time as she undid the buttons, happy, it came as a shock to Collins when he heard her gasp.

"Ah, don't bother about that. It was just an accident," he said, watching the girl's accusing face.

But the mood had passed. There was no escape from the violence of the last few days. The thin angry line of flesh came between them as effectively as his earlier jealousy and despair.

She wanted to know, she demanded to know what had happened. Somehow Collins felt no pleasure in her anxiety, only a feeling of irritation at having to waste time on explanations that couldn't possibly affect her. What was done was done, and the hell with it.

So they sat on the edge of the bed and Collins lit cigarettes and told her everything from start to finish. When he had stopped talking they sat in silence for a while, listening to the steady chirp of the night-insects and the voices in the patio outside.

"This being a sailor—does it mean so much, then, to you?" she asked finally.

"It's my life—or, rather, was my life," Collins said, leaning back on the pillows, feeling relaxed and quiet now that he had said it all aloud.

"But the boy—why should you feel so bad about him? It wasn't your fault."

"Oh, I don't know," Collins yawned. I'm not sure about anything any more, he thought, watching the girl as she moved her head absently. "And what about your troubles?" he said lightly, pretending a gaiety he didn't feel. He wondered what the time was.

"That poor boy," she said, taking no notice of the question. "Will they pay the fine for him?"

"What fine?" Collins sat up. "I didn't hear anything about a fine."

"Ha!" She grimaced, picking up a brush from the small

dressing-table. "There is always a fine. They prefer to have the fine paid. Otherwise they will put him in the prison." She looked at him in the mirror. "Do you know what it is like in the prison?"

"No, and I don't want to," Collins said angrily, standing up. "Christ, I'm hot!" The evening breeze had dropped, and it felt close and stuffy in the room.

"Would you like a shower?" the girl asked. She opened one of the drawers in the table and took out a towel. Looking over her shoulder, Collins saw the photograph of a dark-haired boy. He looked about four years old, standing with his arms round the neck of a big dog.

"He yours?" Collins asked quietly.

She nodded. She held the photo in her hand, studying it. "He is like me—no?" She put it back in the drawer.

"Where is he now?"

"He is at school. A military school. It is very expensive." She turned, looking at him aggressively, half smiling. "That is why I must have important friends in the Army."

Collins grinned. He wanted to ask her how much she thought the fine would be on Yellow Shirt, but he didn't want to go back to all that again. The ship would be leaving tomorrow. He had decided to stay the night, since he knew that the "friend" wouldn't be coming. This might be the last good time he had waiting him for a very long while ahead.

Collins stood holding the girl for a moment when she had switched off the light; then she opened the door and he followed her to the showers, which were just along to the right, built into a corner of the patio.

9

LATE THAT NIGHT, or rather, the next morning, Collins woke in sudden terror. An animal was rooting around under the small barred window set high in the wall opposite the bed. He woke quickly, instantly, as does a sailor used to working on watches. The animal moved off after a while—some dog, Collins thought—and he lay on his back, the girl sleeping peacefully in the crook of his arm, looking out the window at the sky. The stars were fading over the sea, and it would soon be light. There was no sound from the patio, and he lay there, feeling the pumping of his heart gradually slowing down again. He tried to remember if he had been dreaming— some nightmare, perhaps, to account for the fear that even now he couldn't seem to shake off.

I'm getting soft, he thought, feeling the light, warm rise and fall of the girl's body against his side. Some old cur sniffs under the window and I nearly pass out. I wonder how little Yellow Shirt is doing. He remembered the boy as he had last seen him—face down, being dragged out of the bar by the Guards. No, don't think of that now, feeling his heart catching up again like one of the rusty old winches on the ship; this is no time to think of that. He tried to concentrate on the sky through the window. Think of old voyages, he told himself, think of how it was walking up the different streets from the docks where you've been. Think of the way the land smells out at sea before you can even see the coast. Concentrate on all the good times.

He tried hard, but it was no use. He turned his head slowly, looking down at the girl's black hair. She slept like a cat, resting her cheek on a hand, knees drawn up, the other arm lying over his shoulder. Watching her, Collins felt himself slowly gripped by the panic he had awakened to. That Mate, he thought. That dirty, lousy, stinkin' Mate. He saw clearly how not only had he lost his job, his way of life, but now also this girl. There was nothing he could do or have now that he wouldn't lose very soon. At this moment, more than any other, he had a glimpse of how it could have been. A steady berth, regular runs down here, Svensson and Mickey and the rest of them, and now this girl. He would have been able to come here often, see her whenever they were in port—"friend" or no bloody "friend."

He could have been even luckier than he had imagined, standing on top of that hill in the cold morning, looking down at the ship. He must have stirred or made a sound involuntarily, because the girl woke then.

She smiled, touching the corner of her eye with a finger.

"You can't sleep?"

She pulled his head down to her neck. She looked surprised when he drew back.

"What's the matter?" she asked.

Collins lifted himself up, put his hands on her shoulders, looked down into her face.

"Listen. Now, listen carefully. How much do you like me? Would you go away with me?" The words sounded fatuous even to himself. He felt her stiffen under his hands.

"Go away with you" she said. "Where? No—let me up. Are you serious? What is the matter with you?" she said, sitting up now.

"Nothing's the matter. Look," he said desperately, "is it so terribly hard to understand? I love you. And this is the last chance I have to see you." He saw the relaxed, resigned look of pity come into her face, the rather bored look of one who had probably heard this many times before, possibly at this very hour. And he hurried on quickly. "Listen to me. I *mean* it. Wouldn't you like to get away from this? I mean . . ."

He wasn't reaching her. He tried again. "I've nothing to go back to when I leave this. I've nothing left except broken-down jobs I could never stand. I can't face going through all that again. And there's you. I want you, to stay with you. Is that so hard to understand? You think I'm crazy because I've only seen you twice? Slept with you twice? Well, how many times do I have to see you before I can say I love you? Do I have to see a girl some special number of times before I can say that?" Her small sleep-lined face watched him seriously as he went on whispering urgently. "And your son, there. Are you going to work at this business all your life? You have to stop some time. You know that." He paused, searching her face. "You like me some, don't you?"

She nodded. "*Sí.* I like you very much." She relaxed, leaning against him. "Yes, very much. But it is impossible, what you say."

"Impossible? Why impossible?" But he said it with no conviction.

The girl put her arm round him, stroking his back. "Because I must work here to keep my son. Because it would be impossible for you to stay in this country. Because—oh, because you ask too much. You ask me to leave here, to go away with you—when you say you do not even have a job. How can you ask such a thing like that? Of course I would like to leave here—to get away from all those fat, drunken pigs—but where do you think we would go?" She spoke consolingly, her voice muffled against his chest.

Collins dropped back on to the bed. Yes, it was a fine dream, wasn't it? he thought bitterly. Some idea! The girl leaned over him, stroking his forehead. She thinks I'm sick. Perhaps I am. His face felt burning.

"What will you do?" the girl asked presently. "Have you no family?"

Collins shook his head. Looking at the girl, he thought: Well, I asked for love, for too much, and this is what I get. Pity. He turned his face to the wall.

"And what about your family?" he asked. "Have you got any family?"

She answered mechanically, as if she was thinking of something else. "A mother, a brother. The boy stays with them when he is not at school. My mother is of this country. My father was Portuguese, you know." She stood up.

Collins lay back on the bed, watching the girl dress. The sky through the window was milky-blue with the early light now. "Your father is dead, then?" he asked. It was important to keep talking.

"I don't know," the girl said, pushing her feet into the high-heeled white shoes. "He came here to grow vines. But the ground was no good, so one day he went away. I was only little then."

"And your brother? What does he do?" And the other part of him was thinking—I won't have a cent when we get back north. I'll have to wire Anne for the car-fare. The hell I will, he raged, I'm not crawling back on my hands and knees to her, to that room. There must be some other way.

92

". . . and he has a small *estancia* there. I will take the boy there when I am finished here," the girl was saying. "What? Where did you say he lived?"

She repeated the name of the adjoining country.

Ah—what's the use? Collins thought, relaxing again. It would take more money than you've ever seen. He got up and started dressing.

"Would you like some breakfast?" the girl asked when he was ready.

"As long as we don't have to go out and hunt it up in the desert first." Collins grinned at her. "Breakfast! It's not that curry stuff, is it?"

She laughed. "No. Eggs and coffee. We are quite civilized here really." She stood very close to him, with the soft look in her face again. "Good-bye," she whispered.

Collins kept grinning, holding her tightly. "If—just 'if,' mind you—I was rich, had enough money for it," he said, as if he were teasing her, playing some kind of game. "If I had money, would you come away with me to that place your brother's got? I mean, if it were possible to buy visas—all that kind of thing. Would you do that—would you?"

The girl was so long in replying that it seemed to Collins, standing there holding her, that she wasn't ever going to answer.

And then, "Yes," she said very quietly. "Yes, I think I would. If it were possible."

If he had felt badly before, it was much worse now.

"Yeah? And how would we get out of this country? Me—how would *I* get a permit to live there?"

But now it was her turn. "Oh, it could be arranged. There would be work for you on the farm. Anything can be arranged for money in this country, you know."

"So I imagine." Collins was in a panic to be gone now, to end this conversation with its false hopes.

The girl looked up at him quickly, anxiously, then said, in the old teasing voice: "All we need is the money, eh?" She lifted his hand to her face. "Come. I will cook you something to eat before you go back to the ship," she whispered.

They walked down the deserted patio, hand in hand,

towards the bar. The big tree stirred softly, shaking the little bulbs on its branches. She lifted the flap of the bar and Collins followed her through to the small kitchen behind. The girl worked quickly, and when the food was ready they carried it out to a table in the patio.

They sat in silence while Collins ate, hearing all around them the sounds of sleepers turning over in the beds, breathing heavily, low voices talking.

While they were sitting drinking the coffee, Collins said: "What'll you do if this revolution comes near here?"

"Here is the safest place in the country. They don't ever come here. Why should they destroy us when we make them so much money?"

"And the general. What'll happen to him?"

"If the Army is successful, then he *will* be a general. *Oye!* And what a general! Already he must change his uniform every day." She laughed. It sounded forced.

Collins said quietly, slipping it in: "And you? You'll marry him?"

It was as if he had struck her. Her body sagged, her face twisted miserably. "I may have no choice," she said. "Why did you say that? Did you not understand that already?" Her shoulders started shaking and she was crying. "And you talk of going away with me when you can do nothing," she said fiercely.

She got up, standing away from him, her mouth still trembling. "Go now, please. Before the others get up." She saw the look on Collins's face as he moved towards her and said quickly: "No—just go now."

When Collins got to the door he looked round once before going outside. He couldn't see her face clearly from here. The girl was standing as he had left her, watching him, her arms hugging her body like a child. She didn't move or say anything, so he went out, closing the big door behind him.

He found a taxi-driver sleeping in the back seat of a big Cadillac, and he woke him up and got him to drive back to Bienvida. The early-morning sun glared into their faces as they drove through the desert, and Collins closed his eyes. He felt empty and very much alone.

A few shops were open in the square as they passed round it, but there didn't seem to be many people up yet.

A woman was milking a goat just beside the statue, and a group of people were standing outside the open window of a store. As the taxi went past, Collins heard the fast, slurring chatter of a man's voice coming over the radio. Then they were out of the square and driving down the road to the dock gate. Collins motioned to the driver not to stop at Michael's Bar but to go straight on to the ship. He didn't feel like having to listen to the little man's troubles this morning.

Four Guards were standing by the gate. They unslung their short automatic rifles when they saw the taxi coming. One of them walked towards the taxi holding his rifle in both hands, jerking the barrel to make them stop. Collins saw that the other three had spaced themselves round the wire gate. When the driver had stopped, the Guard walked round and looked in the window. Collins handed him his pass. The Guard grunted something, then opened the door on Collins's side. Collins got out and stood in the road. The other three Guards came up then and began to search him. One of them went behind him, feeling in his hip pocket. Collins could hear him turning over the paper money he still had left, counting it. When they had gone through all his pockets, they went and looked in the taxi. The driver didn't say anything. He got out and stood in the road on the other side of the taxi, watching the Guards. He looked bored. When they had finished searching the taxi, the Guard who had been holding Collins's money in his hand all this time came and stood in front of Collins, grinning.

The other three Guards were also grinning now. They stood on one side, watching. The Guard with the money licked his thumb deliberately and peeled off four notes, looking and grinning at Collins as he did this.

*"Propina*—no?" he said.

Then he gave Collins the rest of the money. All four of them stood in a row grinning as the taxi drove through the gate and down to the ship. There was enough money left to pay the taxi-driver and give him his *propina*—his tip.

All it needs now, Collins thought, is for old Gold Teeth to bum a cigarette. But he was past caring about what these Guards did any more. In a few hours they would be at sea, heading for Ferragas, then north. Why worry about a few notes anyway?

There was no sign of either Gold Teeth or his relief on deck. As Collins walked aft he could hear the crew's voices and the clatter of plates as they ate breakfast. He had missed the first hour's work, but nobody was going to worry about that now. He hoped the coffee would still be hot. And if Mickey's got any booze, I'll have a shot of that too, he thought. I certainly need it this morning.

His cabin door was open, and as Collins came down the companionway he could see Mickey still flaked out on his lower bunk. Svensson looked at him gloomily when he went into the mess-room.

"How's that coffee, Svensse?" Collins asked, leaning across the table to cup his hand round the pot. Even the Greeks looked as though they had hangovers this morning. He picked up the pot, looked round for his mug.

"Two thousand dollars American on the boy."

"Uh?"

"The fine is two thousand dollars for Yellow Shirt." Svensson kept his head down. He didn't look at Collins. "The agent came down last night and told the Old Man. They had put him in that jail near Ferragas."

Collins poured three quarters of a mug of coffee and went into his cabin. There was a half-bottle of white rum standing on the table. He poured a big shot into the coffee and sat down on the bench under the porthole.

*Two thousand bucks!* That must be the price they set on the dignity of one of those monkey-men. *Two thousand!* He used both hands to bring the mug up to his mouth.

Mickey stirred and opened his eyes.

"That you, Big Jay?" His voice sounded cracked, and he squinted at Collins, shielding his eyes with a hand. "You heard about the fine?" he asked, clearing his throat. He looked shaky and pale.

"Svensse just told me. You think the company will fork out?"

"Not a chance. Jesus, I feel like a crippled dingo this morning," Mickey groaned.

"How long does he get if they don't pay the fine?" Collins asked.

"Christ knows." Mickey turned his head away from the light.

Collins sat drinking the coffee and rum. When he had finished it he went back to the mess-room and got some more coffee, then came back into the cabin again and spiked it with the rum. Mickey was sitting on the edge of the bunk now, holding his head in his hands.

"You goin' to be all right for the let-go?" Collins asked.

"I don't know and I care less. I spewed my stomach up in the night, but I still feel terrible. I tell you, Big Jay, I'm sick of this ferry-boat. I meant what I said about paying off."

"What'll you do then?" Collins asked.

"I don't know. I thought maybe I'd go out to the Coast and try for a ship back to Aussie."

"What about your wife?"

Mickey shrugged. He looked over at Collins. "And it seemed such a good idea gettin' married." He laughed. "You remember how it was at the end of the war, Big Jay, with everybody paying off and going ashore? When you could get almost any berth you wanted? Well, that was the time I got married. My ship was up the Gat then, having repairs, and I'd known this girl for some time. My God, cobber—it looked so bloody easy then. Get married, a few more trips, then we'd have enough money to go back to Aussie in style." He paused. "Instead of which I'm still sitting here on this stinkin' tub, sending home allotments to the wife, but never got enough to clear off and make the start!"

Collins thought for a moment. "You mean you're goin' to clear out—cut adrift from your wife?"

"Well, why not? What good's she doin' me there in Denmark? Ah-h, that's just the hell of it. She's a good kid. You can't blame her for not wanting to come back to Aussie. When we got married, the idea was I made a few more trips just to get a stake together. She don't want to be stuck out there in Aussie with me away at sea." Mickey stood up. "I'm goin' to be sick again after that lot," he muttered. He went up the companionway unsteadily. When he came down again he looked a little better.

"Let's have a shot of that," he said, picking up the

rum-bottle. He took a swallow, then passed it to Collins.

"No. I don't want any more of that stuff," Collins said. "We'll be throwing on those hatch covers pretty soon now."

"You heard what time we're sailing?" Mickey asked.

"Some time early this evening."

"I wonder if that Mate will be on deck."

"The hell with the Mate. He'd better keep outta my way," Collins said angrily. "What's this Ferragas place like, anyway?"

"Nothing there except a jetty. They bring the sugar down by train. The sugar plantations used to belong to a European company, but these thieves confiscated the lot. It's hotter than Queensland up there. Mud flats all along the coast. Tide goes out for miles." Mickey took another swallow from the bottle.

"Well, one things's for sure," Collins said quietly. "We'll go up and see the kid while we're there."

Svensson came in from the mess-room. Collins moved over to make room for him on the bench.

"You have a good time last night, Big Jay?" Svensson asked, sitting down.

Mickey grinned. "Yes, tell us how you made out, cobber." His eyes were like red glass.

"It was nothing special." Collins didn't want to talk about the girl. What was there to say, anyway? "Fish-net sent her love to you, Svensse," he said, trying to make a joke.

He thought of the girl standing there by the table, crying. Listening to Mickey talking about his wife, he had made up his mind that he wasn't going back to Anne. He tried to think what he would do when he paid off, but he could imagine nothing beyond that station at the bottom of the square in Bradport. The best thing to do, he told himself, was not to think that far ahead yet. He had managed to keep his hope alive all through those two years ashore, but now he knew this would be his last voyage. He didn't try to kid himself any longer about that. What happened to him when he went ashore for the last time was of no importance. That would take care of itself.

"How long will it take to get to Ferragas?" he asked, hoping they wouldn't talk about the girl again.

"We leave tonight, we get there tomorrow morning, I think," Svensson said. "It's only just over one hundred miles. Two days to load the sugar. Then back to the north."

Don't think about the girl. "How did Cookie take the news about the fine?" Collins asked.

"I think he has some idea of trying to pay it off himself with his savings," Mickey said. "Only he hasn't got enough. May take up a collection among the kid's relatives. We all said we'd throw something in. Two thousand is going to take some collecting."

"What surety you got that they'll let the kid go when you've paid this fine?" What can *you* put in? he thought. Nothing. I already owe Svensse just about all my wages to the end of the trip.

"They'll spring him, all right," Mickey said, turning the nearly empty bottle around in his hands. "They don't want to ruin a good racket. They've got enough savvy for that, you bet." He finished the last half-inch of rum. "I wish to Christ somebody would take up a collection for me so's I could buy that taxi."

They heard the sounds of the stevedores as they came up the gangway on the deck. Collins and Svensson stood up. Svensson looked worried.

"Take it easy, Mickey," he said as they went out of the cabin.

"The hell with you, you ole squarehead. Why should I worry?" Mickey laughed and lay back on the bunk again.

# 10

THE PILOT came aboard just after six in the evening. They had finished unloading before tea. The iron cross-beams had been laid across the hatches, and the derricks had been lowered, ready for sea. The hatch covers would be thrown on after they had got under way. The Old Man had been on deck all afternoon. The word had gone round that the Army had won a victory somewhere in the west. Nobody, of course, was exactly sure how much of a victory it was or even how far away in the west. But the Old Man was anxious to take the ship out of it. Ferragas was near the border, and they would be there only a short time. And, from what Collins had heard about the place, there didn't seem to be much there worth fighting over. He only hoped they would be able to dig up some kind of taxi to take them out to the jail to see Yellow Shirt.

The Mate came out on deck for the letting-go. He wore a silk muffler round his neck. His face was still swollen, and his eyes were very bloodshot. When they had taken the lines in, instead of the usual shout "All-ll gone for'-ard," he waved to the Old Man on the bridge. He neither spoke to, nor looked directly at, Collins.

When the crew had flaked the lines out along the deck, they leaned over the shore rail. The tide was just starting to ebb, dragging with it out to sea the line of oily scum, cigarette-ends, and flotsam that had fouled the water between the ship and the dock. Collins noticed that the wire dockgate had been closed and the Guard was not in the sentry-box. The four stevedores who had let go the lines off the shore bollards had filed away behind one of the warehouses. The whole area was now empty, deserted, desolate. It was the saddest-looking port he had ever sailed out of.

The next morning, after he had come off watch at four o'clock, Collins went down to the galley for some coffee. Mickey was sitting on the table. He said: "I could sleep a week."

"Well, if you're signing off, I don't suppose it matters much," Collins said, pouring himself some coffee. He felt tired and irritable himself. During the last four hours he had gone over everything time after time—the fight, Yellow Shirt, the girl. He had tried thinking what would have happened if he had acted differently—above all, if he hadn't had the fight with the Mate. He felt very sure now that both the other bad things hinged on that. He told himself that, for a man who had just had the first luck in two years, he had acted like a lunatic. And he would lean forward over the wheel or, if he was on the fo'c's'le-head, punch his hand hard against the winch-drum, feeling desperate, physically sick. He leant back now against the bulkhead in the galley, pressing the back of his head against warm iron.

"You told the Chief you're payin' off?" he asked Mickey.

"No. To tell you the truth, I've been thinking it over." Mickey looked at Collins sheepishly. "I mean, I don't know about cutting off from the wife like I said. It must have been the rum talking. I figure that at least I got some chance of making a go of it if I stick here." He got up and stood with his back to Collins, looking out the porthole. "If I cleared off now, I wouldn't ever get to see her again."

"Sure," Collins said. "I understand. I'd be the same myself. Believe me, I'd have held this old tub down till she fell to bits if I'd had the chance. There's nothing for me ashore."

Just that one slap did it, he thought. I could have stuck it out if he hadn't hit me. I couldn't take that.

"Do you think you'll get another ship?" Mickey asked.

Collins shook his head slowly. "No. Not any more. We got ten times more crews than ships now, and I haven't got the capital to bum around the ports waiting for a chance on a foreign line. No, I'm through now. It was a lucky break, I thought, when I got this berth."

All I needed, he thought, was a few trips to get a little stake together and I could have pulled that deal with the girl. She meant that, all right, about shoving off to her brother's place.

"Well, I'm going to turn in," he said aloud.

"Yes, me too, cobber. Hey, by the way, when are you planning to see Yellow Shirt?"

"Today, of course. Straight after tea. We'll take some cigarettes—stuff like that." Collins looked at Mickey. "Why—what's the matter? You don't want to go or something?"

"No. No. It's not that. Only, you're not planning to try anything silly, are you, Big Jay? I mean—" He hes-

101

itated, studying Collins's face. "You been acting pretty jumpy these past couple of days."

Collins grinned. "Well, for Chrissakes!" he said softly. "What did you think I was going to do? Try and crash the jail single-handed?"

"No. Only, you'd better watch yourself. I mean, don't start goin' off half-cocked at one of the Guards when we get there."

"You think I'm crazy yet?" Collins said. Then he went to his cabin.

After breakfast they were in sight of the coast again. The mountain chain had broken away some time in the night, and here the shore was a long, low, flat line. The pilot boat pushed its way out towards them through still, muddy-coloured water. A flock of seabirds was screaming over some ripples that concealed a bar. There was no wind this morning, and once the sun was up it was hot and airless.

The crew stood by on the fo'c's'le-head as the ship swung and manoeuvred through the shallow water. Even at high tide the surrounding banks and spits of mud were scarcely covered. They passed through there, going very slow, the engine-room telegraph constantly ringing, and then they were in deeper water. Collins saw how the mud bars and banks came out from the coast, circling out to sea, making where they were now a natural harbour. As they approached the land, Collins could see a high, wide jetty sticking out, with a small coaster tied up on one side, close to the shore.

The ship slowly nosed her way alongside the jetty. Looking over the bows, Collins saw the dirty water slope up to the shore. Another few yards and they would have scraped the bottom. He squatted down to bend a bowline in the heaving-line round the big spliced eye laying on the deck. As he straightened up again, he heard a sharp piping whistle, and a small train came running down the tracks laid along the jetty, shunting a row of open iron trucks loaded with sugar sacks in front of it. A man stood on the end of the jetty, waving the driver on carefully. When the train had stopped, the stevedores got down from where they had been sprawling on the sacks and stood waiting for the gangway to be put out.

"Pretty quick work, hey?" one of the Greek sailors said.

"Damn quick, I'd say." Collins looked across to where the coaster was tied up on the other side of the jetty. She was a single-deck ship, two hatches, the wheelhouse at the stern. Her bows were pointing out to sea. There were two Guards on the deck, but Collins couldn't see any crew. He followed the others down to rig the gangway. The first man aboard was another Guard. He looked much older than the others Collins had seen, and he smiled almost apologetically as he stepped on to the deck.

Mickey came up from the engine-room and stood leaning over the side. "My God, you could fry an egg down below," he said. He still looked shaky from his big drunk. "What's the coaster doing?" he asked, wiping his face.

"Don't know." Collins coiled one of the derrick guys on to the hatch. "It's one of theirs, I think."

The stevedores came aboard, and pretty soon the winches were rattling and the first sacks were going down into the holds. They worked with some speed here, all right, Collins thought.

The Mate had gone back to his cabin, and the Second put the crew on some light work, painting and cleaning round the crew's quarters. It was so hot every movement made them pour with sweat. The dirty water gave off a rotted smell, as if they were up some creek instead of out on the coast.

After tea it was still very hot, and they missed the shade the mountains had thrown over Bienvida at this time of day. Cookie got finished as quick as he could, and then he and Collins and Mickey and Svensson went ashore to try to find some way of getting up to the jail. The stevedores had been relieved, and another gang was going to work through the night. Every so often the empty train would pull away from the jetty, and there would be that small shriek of the whistle, and another one would run up alongside the ship. They were really throwing those sugar sacks down now.

The four of them went down the gangway, edged between two of the trucks, stepping over the rails, and walked along the jetty towards the town. They were just passing the bows of the coaster when a truck came down over the slight incline of the road leading on to the jetty. The whole thing was packed with Guards. It drew up opposite the deck of the coaster, which was level with the jetty. Guards jumped down from the back and, forming a cordon, began to pass green wood boxes out of the truck into the coaster. Two men who appeared to be officers directed the operation. One of them looked round as the four seamen came near, then turned away again.

"Look at them work, will you," Mickey said. "I didn't know those boys ever did any of that. What d'you suppose is in those boxes?"

"Rifles, looks like to me," Collins said. He was feeling nervous now about seeing Yellow Shirt. "They're about the right shape."

"Maybe it's their second-front offensive they're going to launch from here," Mickey said.

When they got to the top of the slight incline the narrow railway branched into a double track. There was a town here, small and dirty-looking, and all around it Collins could see the desert stretching out for miles. The whole place looked and smelt like the end of the world.

Collins stood outside the only bar, waiting while the others enquired about a taxi. He had brought along four cartons of cigarettes and all the money he had left wrapped up small in a piece of oilskin. He was trying to think out what he was going to say to the kid. The sun was going down, looking like a big red boulder blocking the end of the street. A rat scuttled round a pile of garbage.

The others came out of the bar presently. Mickey was carrying a couple of bottles of rum. A fat little man in a stained vest came waddling out behind them and disappeared round the back of the building.

"Ole Grease-top is going to run us out himself," Mickey said. He unstoppered one of the bottles and passed it round. Everybody took a big drink except Cookie. He stood to one side, staring between his feet.

The fat man drove a beat-up car round to the front,

and they all piled in. Cookie hunched up in one corner, looking very dark and miserable. Nobody said anything, but Mickey kept passing the bottle round. The fat man took his share, and Collins gave him a packet of cigarettes. Collins had been worrying about whether they had visiting-hours at the jail, and he thought that they might need any influence the fat man, as sole bar-keeper in the place, might have.

As they rode out through the desert, the sun was in their eyes all the way and the air was stifling. The country up here was flat, like Bienvida, but more tropical-looking. They passed pools of stagnant water and short, scrubby-looking trees and a very tall kind of grass. The car lurched over the road, banging them from side to side. It was getting dark now, and besides the usual cricket and grasshopper noises Collins could hear the steady monotonous hissing of mosquitoes. It was the most God-forsaken, fever-looking country he had seen since he had been to West Africa years ago, when the ship he had been in had loaded fish-meal. He waited now, with a patient hollow terror, to see what the jail would be like.

But they didn't have to go all the way out to the jail. They had been travelling for about an hour, slumped in their seats, not speaking, when the driver suddenly slowed down. The car stopped, the noise of the engine ticking over, blending with the mosquito hum, and the driver pointed through the windscreen.

At first Collins couldn't see anything. The night was spreading down over the land, and his eyes were blurry from riding straight into the now dying sun. Then, away across on his side, he saw a line of figures, seemingly no higher off the ground than the backs of dogs or small animals would be. The four of them got out of the car, and the driver switched off the engine.

"Looks like a string of donkeys," Mickey said, peering into the gloom.

Collins didn't reply. He reached into the car and brought out the four cartons of cigarettes.

"Those aren't donkeys," Svensson said. "I think they are men." The ground on this side sloped up slightly towards the figures in the distance. There were no trees or cacti or any growth of any kind except small clumps of spiky grass.

Their feet scuffled in the stony barrenness of the ground, and the clumps of grass brushed against their legs with a dry rattling sound as they started walking forward in a line, straining to see ahead of them. When they were about one hundred yards from the indistinct shapes Svensson coughed, and one of the dark humped figures straightened up, and they saw it was a man. He was evidently in some kind of ditch, because his body was visible only from the waist up. The man appeared to be staring at them, but they were unable to make out his face. They were walking now through an almost solid cloud of mosquitoes that settled on Collins's face and neck in a stinging rash. They were quite close to the man, and one by one the other figures heard them coming and straightened up and watched.

The four seamen stood now looking down at the line of men who were dredging out a ditch. The men were standing almost knee-deep in black, oily-looking liquid. They leaned on the wooden pick-handles, nobody speaking, in the attitude of men grateful for any kind of interruption to break off work. Collins looked for the boy among the dark, bite-swollen faces of the prisoners, some of whom were to exhausted to lift their heads even to see who had come across from the road. Looking along this line, Collins saw that the ditch they were working extended into a wide swamp over to the right which had been hidden to them from the road. Suddenly Collins heard a shout at the end of the line and one of the figures waved.

The four seamen started forward, past the bowed heads, like officers inspecting a file of crippled soldiers.

"Hello, Big Jay. I think perhaps you would come."

It was Yellow Shirt, all right. The cheerful tone of his voice shocked Collins somehow even more than finding him here. Behind the boy the surface of the swamp shone dully in the fading light. Collins squatted on his heels, pausing for a moment to be sure his voice would sound right when he spoke. The boy was smiling at the three seamen standing behind him.

"What you doin' here, kid?" Collins said finally.

"This is where we work. We clear the swamp," the boy said simply. They had taken away his beloved shirt, Collins noticed. He was dressed in some kind of sacking with red hoops. The jacket had no sleeves. The boy looked very small, still grinning at them cheerfully through the living veil of mosquitoes which darkened his face.

My God, why doesn't somebody say something? Collins thought agonizedly. "Look, kid—I brought some smokes," he said, holding out the cartons. "Can you reach?"

"You have to throw them, Big Jay." And the boy lifted his leg and Collins saw the black, glistening chain round his ankle. The movement seemed to break the horrified trance of the three standing behind Collins. Mickey swore and dropped onto his knees. Cookie sat down quickly, crying into his hands.

Collins was aware of the silent line of prisoners, like a set of figures carved from one block, standing watching them. He saw that Mickey was about to say something, and gripped his arm warningly.

"Where's the guard, kid?" Collins said, keeping his voice soft, trying not to show how frightened he was.

"He is away somewhere. He doesn't like these mosquitoes. Nor do I." The boy grinned. He looked at Cookie then, sitting on the ground crying, and Collins noticed the doubtful changing expression come into his face.

"How they treating you here?" Collins said quickly. This cheerfulness of the boy—it was as if he were proud of being here.

"I was sick where they hit me." The boy touched his head gingerly. "But it is getting better now." He grinned. It was as if *they* were in the jam and the boy were visiting them.

"This was some fight, Yellow Shirt," Svensson's deep voice said over Collins's shoulder. "That Guard you hit is still walking round in circles."

"That's right," Mickey said. "You can certainly dish it out, kid."

That was better, Collins thought. That was what the kid wanted to hear. They mustn't let him see how they really felt.

"Reminds me of when I was inside," Collins said.

Twice, he thought. For drunkenness. He glanced around, trying to see the guard. But it was too dark even to see the road now.

"You were in prison too, Big Jay?"

"Sure," he said. "Now, look—take these smokes. Shove 'em inside your jacket. It's big enough, you skinny runt. Catch." He tossed the cartons across one at a time.

Svensson untied his shoe-laces. "Here." He tossed them across to the boy. "Tie them round your ankles. Then you can put the cigarettes down your pants."

"Good on you, Svensse," Mickey said. His voice sounded rather high. "That's the first bright idea that ole squarehead has ever had—eh, kid?"

Collins looked round. The other prisoners were chopping at the ditch again. When the boy had finished tucking the cartons of cigarettes away, he looked up at Collins and grinned again.

Collins, trying to put everything he had left of confidence into his voice, said: "You think you'll be able to stand it, kid?" He didn't mention the fine.

"Sure, Big Jay. I get my job back on the ship, won't I?" the boy said anxiously.

"Of course. Look, we'd better be pushing off now. We don't want that guard to see us."

They all stood up. Cookie had stopped crying.

The boy looked at him, then at Collins. He winked. "That Cookie never make a sailor," he said.

When the others had turned away, Collins took out the oilskin pouch of money and tossed it to the boy. "There's not much there, but it may come in useful. Don't let those others see it. Good-bye, kid. I'll look you up some time."

"Good-bye, Big Jay. Don't you worry 'bout me."

Collins turned round once as he walked to catch up the others. The boy waved, and he waved back. Then it was too dark to see him any longer.

As they got back to the car waiting on the road, they saw head-lights coming towards them. They stood watching as a truck pulled up and a Guard got down from the back. He looked over at the car and shouted something to the driver, then started walking towards the prisoners.

He had come to collect them to drive them back to the jail.

The driver of their car seemed anxious to get away. He made signs with his hands showing them that the Guard had told him to clear off. The four seamen got into the car and the driver started back to the ship.

Mickey got out the bottle of rum and passed it round. *"A chain-gang!"* he kept saying. "A kid like that!"

Cookie had started crying again, and Svensson sat staring out of the window.

You can't break someone like Yellow Shirt, Collins thought, watching the car's head-lights jerking and swaying from side to side as they bumped over the road. You can't break someone like that. He was proud to be stuck out in that swamp. It was written all over his face. No, they wouldn't be able to break him now, Collins thought, reaching behind him for the bottle Mickey was offering. But unless someone comes across with that two thousand they're very likely to kill him. All we did was encourage him in his attitude. But what else could I have said? Collins thought.

When they finally got back to the bar, Collins and Mickey waited outside while Svensson went in to settle with the driver. Cookie had stopped crying, and he turned to Collins and spoke for the first time since they had left the ship that evening.

"All that money they have down there. And they want more for the boy."

"What money do you mean, Cookie?" Collins offered him a cigarette.

A man stood in a lighted doorway opposite, watching them.

"All that money they bring down to the ship today. But where can I get two thousand dollars?" He started shaking again. "I know his people haven't . . ."

"What money—what ship?" Collins interrupted, holding Cookie by the shoulders. He looked at Mickey. Mickey looked puzzled.

"On the coaster. The old Guard on the ship told me. They put it on board today. You remember, we saw them. The old Guard told me it was coming. Those boxes were full of money."

109

## 11

THREE GUARDS were sitting on the hatch of the coaster playing cards when they walked back from the bar. A single spot-light at the head of the gangway shone over the Guards. The rest of the coaster was in darkness. Collins looked carefully at the hatches as they walked along the jetty. The covers were on, and the tarpaulins had been dragged across, but they were not battened down. He could see the loose edges hanging over the coamings. One of the Guards looked up from the game as the seamen passed, a brown cigarette dangling from his mouth. Collins stared back for an instant, then looked away.

The four seamen stepped between the trucks of sugar sacks and went up the gangway of their own ship. Cluster-lights had been hung over the holds, and the faces and bodies of the stevedores glistened with sweat in the hot, still air. The old Guard was leaning against the bulwark, his rifle propped up by his side. He smiled at them.

Collins took Cookie by the arm and drew him along the deck towards the stern. They waited while a load of sacks swung up over the side and dropped down into the hold with a rattle. The four of them stood now by the ladder leading up to the poop.

"Now, you understand what I want you do to, Cookie," Collins said urgently. "I want you to go back to the galley and dish something up for that Guard. And find out all you can, but, for Chrissakes, don't show you're pumping him." Out of the corner of his eye Collins could see the Guard chatting to one of the stevedores. "You think you can do that, Cookie?"

Cookie nodded miserably. He looked old, frightened, now. His eyes showed what a beating he had taken today —first the boy, now this. He had accepted the idea when Collins had first told him outside the bar, listening dully, answering Collins's questions automatically.

"O.K., then. Go ahead and do your stuff. Find out all you can."

Cookie turned away and began to walk back along the deck. Collins watched him say something to the Guard, then the pair of them moved off towards the galley.

That's all right, then, Collins thought. He glanced over at the coaster. The Guards were still playing cards. He turned back to the other two, taking no notice of the look on Mickey's face. Svensson just stared at the swinging sacks as they came over the side from the trucks below.

Collins led the way up the poop-ladder and sat on one of the bitts on the stern. Svensson leant against a stanchion, fraying a piece of twine in his hands. Mickey sat with his back against the bulwark, watching Collins. He had opened the other bottle of rum, and they passed it round, not talking.

Collins had a good view of the coaster from here. All he had to do now was watch those Guards. He went over what Cookie had told him. It wasn't much. The old Guard spoke English. He had worked as a foreman for one of the big plantations back in the country when it had been run by foreigners. Just over a year ago the Government had taken over all foreign interests in the country and the Guard was out of a job. So he had joined this outfit he was in now. It was the only kind of job that paid a decent salary in this country. He lived alone in the town, and he liked to talk to foreigners about the good old days when he had been foreman. And he had told Cookie about this coaster, which had been loaded now for several days but had no crew. He had heard the other Guards talking about the delivery of the boxes earlier that day while he had been waiting for the ship to arrive. Something about money. That was all.

It could be just a rumour, Collins thought. But there was something funny about that coaster being there, loaded, with no crew. And he had seen the Guards handling those boxes that he had thought probably contained rifles. He had seen that himself. Why didn't they get the stevedores to handle them? And if . . .

"You're crazy, Big Jay," Mickey burst out, getting to

his feet. "You must be off your head. I know what you're thinking."

Svensson tugged at the piece of twine. "They shoot you full of holes before you even get up the gangway," he said softly.

Collins looked at them both.

Mickey stood in front of him, his fists clenched. "You'd never do it. How the hell you think you're goin' to even get one foot on that deck with all those Guards there?"

"I didn't say anything yet, did I?" Collins said, looking at the coaster. "Take it easy till Cookie gets back. I was just interested—that's all."

Mickey stared at him for a moment longer, then snorted disgustedly and sat down again, watching Collins.

They were still sitting there when Cookie came aft about half an hour later. He was carrying a pot of coffee. Collins waited while Svensson went down to the messroom and brought up their mugs, then said: "Well, what did he have to say?"

Cookie started speaking in a low voice, not looking at anyone.

"He says he is sure now it is money. He says those other Guards we see unloading the boxes from the truck did not come from this town. He says they belong to the President. They are his Special Guards. He says they could not be rifles. What would the President want with rifles in another country? He says he thinks the Army is winning and soon the President will have to leave. He says he is sure it must be money because they have sent away the other town Guard who was on the ship before the boxes came. Why should they want three of the President's Special Guards there if it wasn't money?" Cookie paused. "I couldn't find out anything else."

Collins felt a violent pounding in his chest and suddenly realized he had been holding his breath while Cookie had been reciting in that dull, tired voice all he had learned.

"You did very well, Cookie. That's what I wanted to know." Collins put his arm round Cookie's shoulders. "Why don't you turn in now? You look whacked."

Cookie got up, and they watched his small, bowed back as he walked to his cabin. Not once had he wanted to know what all this questioning was about. He seemed

112

to be in a dull, shocked condition, moving around like a machine.

"Well, what about it now?" Mickey said. "You any the wiser now?"

"Maybe," Collins said, grinning slightly. "You two look like you're goin' to throw nervous fits any minute." He stood up, dusting the seat of his pants with his hands. "You comin' up to the bridge with me?"

He took no notice of their questions, and started down on to the deck. The other two followed silently. The noise from the winches and the stevedores shouting covered them as they climbed up past the Old Man's quarters on to the bridge. The wheelhouse door was not locked, and Collins slid it back gently and they went inside. The lights from the deck below guided Collins's way into the chartroom to where the binoculars were kept. He glanced at the ship's chronometers.

8.58 P.M.

The three of them stood round the engine-room telegraph in the wheelhouse, and Collins swept the binoculars first out across the water, then, getting them into focus, directed them on to the deck of the coaster. The three Guards were still sitting there. They had stopped the card game, and one of them was laughing at something. Collins could see every detail of their faces under the gangway spot. He moved the glasses, training them all around the deck, the fo'c's'le-head, the wheelhouse aft. Everywhere was dark and still.

"How does she look?" Mickey said. He sounded different now, not impatient or scornful any longer. It was as if, Collins thought, lowering the glasses for a moment, it was as if he had made up his mind about something.

"Quiet, very quiet. Here, take a look." They waited silently until Mickey put down the glasses.

"Ah—I still think it's crazy," Mickey said. He offered the glasses to Svensson. Svensson shook his head and turned his back to the window.

He doesn't want any part of this, Collins thought, looking at the big man. I don't blame him, either.

He took the glasses again, this time moving up the jetty to where the road lifted out of sight, then round the dark blankness of the coast to the right, thinking as he

113

moved the glasses, adjusting the focus carefully, how this was the only way now; he was going through with it whether the other two came in with him or not. He was getting another chance, and he must do it the best way he could—only getting the money was important now, firstly for the boy, then for him and the girl. I do this right, he thought, excited but feeling confident again, I do this right and there'll be no going north for me. What have I got to lose, anyway?

Looking across and behind the coaster, Collins could see a few lights on the shore. He had noticed there were huts there when they had come in this morning. The shore between the jetty and these huts was a low, out-hanging bank of rock, extending in a curve for about half a mile. Where the huts were this low rock cliff ended, and in front of the huts the beach sloped into the sea. His eyes were getting used to the darkness, and now, in front of the huts, lying on the beach, he could see darker humps. Boats, Collins thought. Must be fishermen's huts. That's why I didn't see the boats earlier today when we came in. They were all out working. He lowered the glasses, turned and looked at Mickey. Mickey stared back at him, silent, expectant.

"How would you do it?" Mickey said quietly. "Tell me that. How would you do it?"

"By the sea," Collins said. "It's the only way." He gave Mickey the glasses, pointing to the huts. "Take a look. Fishermen. Boats. We come in on the blind side in a boat. That's how."

Mickey looked for what seemed a long time. Collins stepped back a pace. Svensson was still standing with his back to the window, hands in his pockets. He must have sensed that Collins was waiting for him to say something. He shook his head.

"I don't think so," he said. "No. You wouldn't do it."

Mickey looked round. "What makes you think you could pull a think like that?" he said. "How can you even be sure it's money?"

Collins shrugged. "It adds up, doesn't it? The Army wins, the President has to go fast. So what does he do? He cleans out the banks. You read about that kind of thing a hundred times. This time next month he'll be in

114

Mexico or Italy or some place with a few million salted away."

Mickey thought for a moment. Another load of sugar sacks dropped into the hold below the bridge with a whining screech as the winch let out the wire. He said: "I thought that too. It adds, all right. But how do you know what kind of cash is in those boxes? What if it's this paper stuff? Or bullion, even? My God—we can't just walk around with gold bars stuck down our pants!"

"I don't know for sure. But I'll bet it's not their own paper stuff. He wouldn't be able to unload that in another country. Bullion he would. But did you notice those Guards when they were unloading that truck? It only took *one* man to handle a box. If it was gold or silver, they would have bust their backs tossing those boxes around. No, whatever was in those boxes wasn't bullion. And, like I say, that stuff they use here wouldn't be any more use to him than tissue paper. So it must be dollars."

Svensson jerked upright at that. "Dollars? You think those boxes were full of dollars? Why, there was a whole truck-load!"

Collins looked at the pair of them standing there in the gloom, very excited now.

"Yes," he said. "Dollars." He paused, letting it sink in. "Look, you heard what that Guard said. Only one year ago they closed down on all the foreign holdings. That means they froze all the cash tied up in the country." He leaned forward in the dark, patting the brass telegraph with his hand. "And not only the dollars from those plantations. A President down in one of these places really runs the show. They got oil, too, haven't they? Since this one's been President, too. How do you think they get paid for that?"

"But how can you tie this in with the President? How can you be sure that old Guard's right?"

"For the very reason he heard anything at all. He was obviously surprised to see those other Guards. And if you think about it you'll remember they *were* dressed different from the others. Their uniforms were different. And what the hell are the President's own mob doing up in this God-forsaken dump? And another thing. Why is there no crew on that coaster? Because what I *think* has

115

happened is that they've got this coaster tied up here, loaded with sugar first, just as a blind. They don't care now whether the people in the town know it's money in those boxes or not. Besides what that old Guard said, I'm willing to bet that everybody in the town knows about it now. But what the hell are they going to do, even supposing the idea of trying to do something did enter their mosquito-bitten brains? Three Guards armed with automatic rifles—for all I know, they got a machine-gun mounted on the fo'c's'le-head and another in the wheelhouse—what could anybody from the town do if they tried?"

"Well, maybe," Mickey said. "You mean you think that President is going to come up here and go off in that coaster?"

"No. Not that way," Collins said slowly. He looked down across to the Guards sitting on the hatch. "No. It's my guess this is just a blind. He'll fly out of the country to one of the other states. Then when he's good and ready this tub is goin' to sail out of here and up the coast to the nearest port wherever he goes. That's why they got her all loaded and with no crew. When the crew does come aboard they won't even know what they're carrying. Or maybe he'll even have some of his own side take the ship up. It doesn't matter which. Once the ship *does* get there, he'll be waiting to meet her, you bet. He's not flying out sitting on those boxes because he's probably not sure what kind of a reception he'll get. Doing it this way, he'll know just where he stands first before the cash arrives."

Collins turned to look directly at Mickey. "For Chrissakes, don't forget that if those boxes are loaded it's not just pin-money. You wouldn't walk into a bar on South Street pushing a few million dollars in front of you in a wheelbarrow. The kind of place this President's goin' to, they'd sell their mothers for a beer. He'll be carrying a big roll for expenses, as it is—enough probably to last you and me a life-time. Don't you see, he wants to be *sure* before he lands all that stuff wherever he's goin'."

"I follow that. But—"

"Hey, look, Big Jay!" Svensson cut in.

Collins looked out of the window quickly and saw two

116

of the Guards coming down the gangway of the coaster. They were carrying something.

"Quick," Collins said, snatching up the glasses. "Go in the chart-room and see what time it is."

He looked through the glasses and focussed the two guards in the big circle. One was carrying a small bucket with a lid. The other had a tray and a pot. Collins watched them turn along the jetty, going towards the town. Then he swung the glasses back, picking up the other Guard who was left on the deck.

"Ten," Mickey said, peering out the window beside Collins. "Just on ten."

Collins saw the remaining Guard stretch and yawn; then, picking up his rifle, slinging it over his shoulder, the Guard walked along the deck and went up the ladder to the after-quarters and the wheelhouse.

"What is it, cobber?" Mickey whispered excitedly. "What are they doing?"

"Just a second," Collins said.

He saw the Guard lean over the side, spit into the water. Then he disappeared round the stern. Collins shifted the glasses over to the other side of the coaster, waiting for the Guard to reappear.

"It must be just on high tide, isn't it?" he asked, keeping the glasses up to his eyes.

"Not yet," Svensson said. "This is no good," he added softly, almost as though he were talking to himself. He stirred uneasily, leaning his arm against the window.

Just then Collins saw the Guard saunter round from the stern. He came down the ladder on the far side, back on to the deck, and walked towards the fo'c's'le-head.

"Where did the other two go?" Mickey whispered. His breath misted over the glass just in front of his mouth.

"They went up to the town. It looked to me like they were going to fetch a meal. It's this other boy I want to watch now."

The Guard was standing on the fo'c's'le-head now, looking over to their ship.

"Get down," Collins said. "Kneel down." The three of

117

them knelt on the wheelhouse matting. "I don't suppose he can even see us, but we better be sure."

They waited till the Guard had turned away and was going down the ladder on to the deck of the coaster, then they stood up again. Collins saw the Guard sit down on the hatch near the gangway again and light a cigarette.

"Well, that's all, for the minute," Collins said, putting the glasses down. "Now all we got to do is see what time those others come back." He felt Svensson grip his arm.

"Big Jay," Svensson said. "I don't know what you think you are going to do. But I tell you this is no good. You will be killed. This is no good," he repeated, shaking his head.

Collins waited some time before replying. "I understand how you feel, Svensse," he said. "But I figure this is my last and only chance. Ever since I came aboard this ship nothing I touched has gone right. I got nothing to go back to," Collins went on evenly. "And I don't intend going back to any lousy shore job again if I can help it. I understand how you feel. I wouldn't think of this if I had a chance to stick aboard this tub. But now I'm fired, and for me that means finished. It was the only thing I cared about doing, and if I can't go on going to sea, then I don't give a goddam. Listen to me, Svensse. The last time I was two years ashore. You ever been two whole years stuck on the beach? And once I finish on this ship, I don't stand another chance. You know that." Collins looked at the big, flat-nosed Scandinavian, the anxious grey eyes. "You know that as good as I do. This is my only chance—mine and the boy's, remember. Because if I get my hands on some of that money, two thousand is for the boy. And if somebody doesn't fork up soon, he's going to be dead out there like a rat up a sewerpipe." Collins looked round quickly to the coaster to make sure the two Guards weren't coming back yet, then went on. "I tell you now that I'm going to try this. Whether you come in on it or not. You don't have to come in, Svensse, nor you, Mickey. But I'm goin' to try it, all the same."

Svensson shook his head, letting go of Collins's arm.

"I can't do it, Big Jay," he said. "No. I think you will be killed."

Collins didn't say anything. He turned and looked down on to the jetty. He wondered how long the other two guards were going to be. It all depended on that now.

"Well," he said finally. "What do you think, Mickey?"

Mickey still had his face close up against the wheelhouse window, looking over to the coaster.

"I don't know," Mickey said. "I think it's impossible too. But how were you planning on doing it, anyway?"

"This time tomorrow night. We sail on the high tide. Those other two Guards have gone up for the supper. When they come back we'll know just how much time we've got. We go ashore, go around over there to where those boats are on the beach, and come in by the sea. That coaster is low enough in the water to be able to get on the deck easily from the other side. You remember they were dumping those boxes in the after-hold close under the wheelhouse. Well, it's my guess they'll have covered them with one, maybe two, layers of bags. If we work fast, we can grab one of those boxes and bring it round in the boat, coming round the front of the jetty, and then take it up on the stern of our ship. Then we'll be away out of here before they even know it's gone."

"But what about that Guard left on the ship?"

"We'd have to drop him. Either wait for him if he took a walk round, like tonight, or come up behind him across the hatches."

Mickey rubbed his hand across his mouth. "Jesus! It's still a big chance, cobber. You mean we'd have to time it to get back on board here just before we sailed? And what about when the other two Guards come back and find their mate? They'll know who did the job then. They'll come after the ship."

"What in? That coaster? Who's goin' to run it?" Collins crossed the wheelhouse and looked at the clock in the chart-room.

10:20 P.M.

"Look," Collins said. "Twenty minutes clear already. All we have to do is ease off one of the covers of the after-hold, slip into the hold, shift maybe a couple of bags, then lift out one box and back down into the boat,

119

go along round the jetty and on to the stern of our ship. The tarpaulins are just laid over the hatches, not battened down. They won't even notice that somebody has been into the hold. And there'll be nobody about on deck here when we get back. The Mate's pulled his big deal at Bienvida, and he won't be around before the letting-go. Any rate, we'll be shielded by the stern. And the Old Man never leaves his cabin in port, you know that."

Mickey grinned nervously. "Boy, you make it sound so easy."

"And how about when the ship is back north?" Svensson asked. "I think there will be six trucks full of police and Customs waiting for you."

Collins shook his head. "I don't think so. If this President is so sure of being chucked out, I don't think he'll be in any position to make much of a squawk. He'll still have more than he can get through in one life-time. No, as I see it, there's only one risk, and that's the Guard. But, you know," Collins said, looking at Mickey, "I believe it could be done without that Guard knowing anything about it. It all depends how long the other two are up in town."

He picked up the glasses again and focussed them on the far side of the coaster, going over the deck and hatches inch by inch.

Mickey nudged his arm. "There they come."

Collins swung the glasses round and picked out the two Guards as they came along the jetty from the town. He could see steam rising from the pot in one Guard's hands. He was carrying a tray with some bread and *tortillas* under the other arm. The other Guard had the covered bucket. Probably stew, Collins thought. Or maybe some of that shrimp curry I had with the girl.

"What's the time now?" he asked, watching the Guards as they went up the gangway. They set the food down on the hatch and Collins saw them take the lid off the bucket and start eating. They were scooping the food between the flat *tortilla* cakes, making sandwiches.

"Ten thirty-five," Mickey said, coming back from the chart-room. A clear half-hour, Collins thought. He put the glasses back in the chart-room, and Mickey and

Svensson followed him down to the deck. Collins leant over the side, watching a piece of driftwood. Just ebbing. Tomorrow night it would be just about high tide at this time.

They walked back towards the crew's quarters. As Collins climbed the ladder, Mickey, just behind him, said: "O.K. I'm with you, Big Jay."

## 12

COLLINS lay on his bunk. The noise from outside on deck penetrated the bulkhead, making it impossible to sleep. Every time a loaded sling of sugar bags bumped against the side of the hold it made a noise like rolling thunder. It was very hot in the cabin, and Collins lay on his back, his arm behind his head, watching the sky through the porthole. He knew Svensson was still awake, he could hear him tossing and turning on the upper bunk.

He's doing more worrying than me and Mickey put together, Collins thought. I think he feels bad about not coming in with us. I don't blame him for that, though —he knows that. It'll be worse for him waiting here. I don't envy him that. Perhaps he'll go up on the bridge like tonight and watch from there. No. He won't do that. Nor would I if I was him. Seeing it all close up through the glasses—how would he feel if he saw . . . ?

No, don't think about that, Collins thought. Fix your mind on the girl, remember all that happened. Yes, that's better. Now work it through from the very beginning, from when you first went into the bar with Svensse and Mickey. Ole Fishnet. I wonder what she's doing right now. Ah, that's a goddam silly thing to think. What the hell you expect her to be doing? Remember how Francesca checked you off on that? My God, what a lot of crap I talked that night!

Maybe she's in there now with some other guy. No. That doesn't mean anything to me one way or another. Just so much work. Well, I get my hands on some of that money and there'll be no more of that. Eddie Simpson! That was the fellow I was trying to remember. The one who got married to that sixteen-year-old in one of the islands. I wonder how he's doing now. Looked happy enough in that photo he sent. Just sitting in front of a bar all day long. I'll bet he's carrying some beer-belly now, though. I must have known half a dozen guys I've sailed with who've settled down here.

Perhaps she was just ribbing you along, Collins thought. No. She was serious, all right. What girl wouldn't be serious about getting out of that place into something better? All she does there is make enough to send her boy to some military school. She told you that herself. She'd jump at the chance if anyone came across with enough money to be able to move her out to her brother's place. Nobody forced her to go to that place, but she'd be glad enough to get away now. If I get a good piece of money, I can fly right back, and we'll move on out. Like in the blues that coloured boy always used to be singing in that mission:

> If Ah had wings like Noah's dove,
> Ah'd fly right back to the girl Ah love.
> Fare thee well, oh honey,
> Fa-are thee we-ell.

I wonder what that boy of hers is like, Collins thought. They're probably training him to be another victorious general like her "friend." I'll bet that "friend" is some fat bastard like that statue up in the square. The hell with him.

Tomorrow night, Collins thought. I've got to do this right. First we get a boat. That's easy enough. We'll start out as though we're heading up to town for a drink, then cut across the country to that settlement along the shore. It'll be good and dark by then. We'll sneak down on to the beach and float a dinghy or something. Not too big. There's sure to be a dinghy there somewhere.

Paddles!

Collins half rose from the pillow. My God, I nearly forgot about that. They're sure to take that kind of movable stuff away at night. Tins. That's what I'll do. Flatten out a couple of tins and use them.

Collins lay back again, wiping a tear of sweat from his nose. I nearly forgot that. Some line, knives, and two flattened tins. By the time we've fixed all that line and tin under our shirts we'll be lucky if we can walk at all. I'll bet we look some sight walking past those Guards.

Collins grinned in the darkness.

No. It's not really so much. We can wrap the tins against our bodies with the line. Won't look no different under one of those loose shirts. Tins, line, knives.

And the piece of pipe I found in the centre-castle, Collins thought. It was about six inches long, with a heavy brass flange at one end. Some engine-room fitting.

But the best way to pull the job would be without having to drop that Guard at all. Do it that way and they mightn't find the box gone until they unloaded the ship. That was the best way. Lift the tarpaulin, case off the hatch cover, one go down under the tarpaulin into the hold, the other lie low watching the Guard on the other side of the deck, then out box, over the side into the waiting boat, and away.

If only there was some fool-proof way of distracting that Guard, Collins thought. If we can do this quietly without the Guard noticing, I believe we'll get away with it. I'll take the pipe, Collins thought, staring up at the deckhead, the excitement of working out the details suddenly gone. I'll take the pipe, but if I have to use it, it'll be all over, everything will go wrong. There must be no more violence. He understood that very clearly now, and he sat up on the bunk, reaching over to his pants pocket for a cigarette.

Svensson moved in the upper bunk. "Give me one too, Big Jay," he said.

"Can't sleep?" Collins asked. In the flare of a match he looked at Svensson's face hanging down over the side of the bunk. He's worrying, all right, Collins thought. He lay back on his bunk.

"I will watch out for you to help you aboard when you come back," Svensson said.

"Will you do that for us, Svensse?" That's the only loose end I had to worry about, Collins thought. "Do

123

you think you can have a ladder ready to let down over the stern? Use the pilot's ladder from the centre-castle. And if anybody wants to know where we are, tell 'em we're up in town. The way I plan it, we'll be back here just before the stand-to for letting-go. That was all I had to think out now—about how to get back on board here."

"I take care of this end, all right, Big Jay," Svensson said. "You don't have to worry about that."

That squarehead, Collins thought. He's been worrying all evening. "You don't have to, Svensse, you know that," Collins said. The big bulge in the mattress over his head shifted uncomfortably.

"That's all right," Svensse said. "But I still think you're crazy. What are you going to do if someone sees you from our ship?"

"Ah—they won't be able to see a thing in the dark. There's only one small gangway spot on that coaster. And when we come back round the jetty we'll keep close in till we cut across the stern of this ship." Collins thought for a minute. "Hey, Svensse—have that ladder ready to let down anywhere over the stern. Don't make it fast till you know for sure which side we're coming up on."

That's everything now, Collins thought, turning on his side. And some time in the early morning, when it got a little cooler, he fell asleep.

# 13

JUST BEFORE nine the next night Collins and Mickey went down the gangway of the ship and started walking up the jetty towards the town. The stevedores had finished loading the sugar sacks, and the ship was ready for sea. The hatches had been battened down, the derricks lowered into their frames, and everything was ship-shape. It had been another hot, cloudless day, and now as they walked up the jetty it was dark and airless.

Collins felt strange, walking with his arms slightly out from his sides, the coiled line and tin under his shirt

making his upper body stiff and hot. He had got two bis-
cuit tins off Cookie and had flattened them in the centre-
castle during the day. The line was an old heaving-line
with the weighted head cut off. They had wound it on to
their bodies down in Collins's cabin just before they
came ashore. The tins had been the most difficult part.
Any way you put them, the sharp edges cut into the flesh.
Finally they had laid them across their backs, covering
them with the line, which reached up to their armpits.
Collins had wanted to take two lines, but it was impossible, and in the end they had had to cut the one line,
Mickey having one half wrapped around him over his
tin and Collins the other. When they were ready they
put on their shirts. It didn't look too bad, and once they
had got past the three Guards on the coaster they weren't
likely to meet anyone else.

So now, walking along the jetty on the side farthest
away from the coaster, pretending to be taking it easy,
just strolling up to town for a drink, they saw the Guards
sitting on the hatch of the coaster playing cards as they
had done last night.

"My God! I feel like a walking hardware-store,"
Mickey said as they got opposite the gangway of the
coaster.

Collins grinned nervously. He was listening to the hollow echo their feet made on the jetty. He was looking
ahead and watching the Guards out of the side of his
eye. One of the Guards looked up then, taking the long
brown cigarette from his mouth, and Collins saw him lean
back and blow a thin jet of smoke towards the lamp.
Then they were past the gangway and Collins could no
longer see anything without turning his head.

"That Guard was giving us the big-eye," Mickey said
under his breath.

"You're just imagining things," Collins said. The
movement had loosened the cord round his body, and he
felt that it was about to fall round his waist. He put
one arm across his chest, holding himself under the other
armpit.

One . . . Two . . . Three . . . Four . . . Five . . .
Not much farther, Collins thought. He strained to hear the
shout, the running feet coming up behind them. It didn't

seem possible that the Guards hadn't noticed anything funny. He looked at Mickey. The sweat was running down Mickey's face like tears. He must be thinking the same thing, Collins thought.

Eight . . . Nine . . . Ten . . . Eleven . . . They were level with the stern of the coaster now.

"Ahhhhhh," came the prolonged cry from behind them.

Mickey almost stopped. Then they heard the slap of a hand of cards being thrown down on the hatch and one of the Guards laughing. Mickey shuddered violently, stumbled forward beside Collins again. Five yards to go now. That noise, Collins thought. It seemed to him that their feet made more noise than a train crossing a bridge. He turned to look at Mickey and immediately felt a sharp stab under his left shoulder-blade. The tin was working loose.

Two more yards, and then they were off the jetty at last, going up the hard earth road alongside the rail track towards the town. The bank sloped up on the right on to the cliff that went round towards where the fishermen's huts were. Collins looked back to the coaster. He couldn't see the Guards from here, only the dark stern. Ahead of them, about a quarter of a mile away, were the lights of the town.

"O.K. Let's go," he said.

They scrambled up the bank, digging their feet into the loose, gravelly sand. There were some low bushes at the top, and they pushed through these, then knelt down, unbuttoning their shirts. They unwound the line from their bodies, panting as if they had been running.

"When that Guard called out I thought we were done, cobber," Mickey said, scrabbling at the line with his fingers.

All around them the bushes seemed alive with the clicking of insects. The line round Collins had dropped into a loose coil over his waist. Another couple of yards and it would have been round my ankles and I'd have fallen flat on my face, he thought. As the line came away, he felt his chest and back run with stinging sweat. It was like wearing a hair shirt. He worked swiftly, coiling the line, taking the loose end round the middle twice and hitching it. Mickey waited, peering through the bushes down the jetty and along the road to the town. Collins could hear him breathing heavily.

When he had finished coiling the line, Collins took the brass pipe out of his pocket. He tied two pieces of rag round each end, not too tight, so they would slip off the thinner end easily. He made three turns round the pipe with these pieces of rag before he made the knots, forming two cushions thick enough to deaden any noise if the pipe slipped out of his pocket on to the iron deck of the coaster. Then he felt around by his feet for the two tin paddles and he was ready.

They got up and, bending forward, started along the low cliff towards the huts. The swishing of the dry grass and the scuffling of their shoes sounded very loud in the still night. They moved at a stooping run, keeping about ten yards back from the edge of the cliff. Once Collins nearly fell headlong into a gulley that opened up suddenly under his feet, and they had to go inland a little way before it was narrow enough to jump across. They were only about two hundred yards from the huts now, and as Collins jumped and landed on the other side of the gulley the tins in his hand clashed.

A dog barked somewhere in front of them, and when Mickey was across they lay flattened on the ground. The dog barked again, and then they could hear it whining over by the huts. Collins took the piece of pipe from his pocket. His heart was pounding violently, and his thighs ached from the stooping run. He put his mouth close to Mickey's ear and said: "Lie quiet. Let it come right up to us."

They could hear the dog sniffing and growling excitedly as it came at them, crashing through the clumps of grass. Collins lifted his head slowly to try to see it. Suddenly the door of one of the huts opened and he saw quite clearly a man standing there, the light from behind him stabbing into the dark. The man waited a moment, then started calling the dog.

Collins put his hand on Mickey's shoulder, pressing gently, meaning him to lie very still. He knew the dog was very near them now, and if it heard a sound, it would start barking.

127

The man in the doorway of the hut shouted again. The dog whimpered, undecided. It sounded to Collins no more than a few yards away. Then the man shouted again, and the dog turned and started back to the hut. Collins lifted his head and after a while he saw the dog cross into the lighted strip coming out of the doorway. The man cuffed the dog, and it ran into the hut. Then the man went inside and shut the door.

Mickey looked at Collins, grinned, and put his hand over his face, shaking his head.

You're not kidding either, Collins thought as they got up and walked forward slowly, so bent their fingers almost touched the ground. I thought that was the finish. I hope there's no more bloody dogs running loose. But it was quite likely, he told himself. They must go very carefully from now on. There was plenty of time.

They were now at the place where the cliff ended and broke down on to the beach in front of the huts. They lay behind the last patch of dry, thin-leafed grass, looking at the boats. Collins counted seven ten-foot fishing-boats. They were of the single-masted, one-sail kind he had seen many times before in these waters. They had been overturned to drain, and the dark shapes looked like small stranded whales. They were of no use because they would be too heavy and large to drag to the water.

Mickey tapped his arm and pointed past the main cluster of upturned boats to one that was a little apart from the rest, and also the farthest away. Collins strained his eyes and thought he saw a smaller, darker object resting against the near side of the boat. He looked at Mickey. Mickey nodded confidently.

Coming out from behind the grass, bending almost double as they went down the exposed slope on to the beach, setting their feet sideways in the loose shale that covered the tops of their shoes, going down sideways now, tensed, nervous, looking all the time towards the huts, waiting for the suddenly opened door, the shaft of light, the barking, growling rush of one of the near-wolf dogs, finally coming on to the flat beach, they crept to the water's edge, making for where they thought the ground would be firmer. But it was even worse here. All loose pebbles. Their feet crunched on the pebbles, sounding as loud as if they were walking on broken glass. They sat down and took off their shoes, knotting them together. Then, cutting back up the beach again, they went towards the line of boats. Using them as shelter, they crossed the open spaces quickly, working along towards the farthest boat. The sharp stones cut and bruised their bare feet, and once they had to wait while a man came out of one of the huts and went into another one.

In the shadow of the last boat in the line they rested, looking across to the one that was apart from the others. Collins could see now that it *was* some kind of dinghy leaned against the overturned hulk. They sat with their backs against the boat they were beside now, waiting till they had got their breath again. The last run across the open beach, all the time expecting to be discovered, had made Collins as tired as if he had just thrown on a complete set of hatch covers by himself. From the way Mickey was gasping beside him, he knew he was in the same shape. There was still plenty of time, Collins thought, looking across the dark, rippling bay towards the ships at the jetty. I have to do this right. I must be exact, he told himself. Now come on. Let's get that dinghy afloat.

Mickey had the coiled line now and one of the tin paddles, and, crouching first, looking again towards the huts, which were very close now, he and Collins made the dash across the last opening to the far boat. Gently they eased the small darkwood dinghy over on to its bottom. Then, one on each side, they lifted it, putting the shoes and tins and line in the bottom under the single seat. It was very light, and in one last rush, feeling the stones tearing the soles of their feet, stubbing their toes, they carried the dinghy down to the water.

Very light, shallow, with broad, curved bows and straight stern, shaped like a seashell, the dinghy was soon bobbing under their hands on the gentle ripples of the incoming tide. They must use it for going over these mud-bars and shallows, Collins thought, as he held it steady while Mickey got in. He took a last look towards the huts, then eased himself over the side.

The dinghy rode very low in the water, and at first they had some difficulty finding the best way to sit in it. The only seat wasn't wide enough for two. So Mickey crouched in the bows, and Collins at the stern, using his greater weight to keep the head up. They started paddling with the flattened tins, using both hands to hold them, one on each side of the dinghy. It was very hot and quiet, and overhead no stars were showing.

They paddled along the cliff, keeping close in to the base. At first it was difficult to make the dinghy steer as they wanted. The broad, curved bows made it twist and turn like a Welsh coracle, and by the time they had crossed the front of the beach and got under the shelter of the low cliff they were nearly exhausted. Neither of them spoke: voices would carry on the water at night.

There was just enough water at the base of the cliff to float the dinghy, and, holding on to a projecting rock, they rested. Mickey's head lolled on his outstretched arm. Collins took in great gulps of the thick, hot air, tired but glad of having worked off some of the nervousness he had felt on the beach. There was a faint breeze coming in from the sea now, and, looking towards the jetty, Collins could see a thin mist rushing past the lights of their ship and making the single spotlight over the coaster's gangway a blurry grey.

Collins nudged Mickey quickly, pointing at the sky and the lights, grimacing his thoughts.

There must be a squall blowing up.

They let go of the cliff then and, paddling furiously, made for the jetty, still keeping well in to the base of the cliff. The incoming tide helped to push them there. They were making better headway with the tin paddles now, and as they reached the place where they would have to leave the cliff and angle across to the coaster, they tried to flatten themselves as much as possible in the dinghy, keeping their faces down, never lifting the bright tin paddles clear of the water.

Collins stopped paddling and, leaning forward, tapped Mickey on the back, indicating for him to look at the time by his wrist watch. 9.44 P.M.

From this point of the cliff to the side of the coaster was about one hundred yards. They were facing towards the stern at a forty-five-degree angle, the wheelhouse aft between them and the Guards. They had the choice of either following on round the cliff till they came to the jetty, that way keeping in the shadow all the time, or cutting straight over to the side of the coaster. This last was the way Collins had planned, and now, looking once again out to sea and feeling the breeze get stronger, he felt it would be best to stick to this idea. The longer way seemed safer, but the time was getting short and he was sure a squall was blowing in. It would be better to be alongside the coaster before it struck.

Mickey looked round at Collins questioningly. Collins nodded his head, pointing to show he thought it would be better to cut straight across. He gestured towards the sky. Mickey nodded, licking his lips. Then they pushed off from the cliff and started paddling towards the coaster.

My God, I hope that squall keeps off a while yet, Collins thought, his face down near Mickey's legs, feeling the weight of the water pushing against the paddle, his arms and shoulders and neck strained and weary. From time to time he raised his head, seeing the dark hull looming slowly nearer. They've only got to come to this side now, to look out to sea for the squall, or just to spit, and we'll be more full of holes than a sieve, Collins thought. They were fighting the tide now, trying to keep the curved bows dead against it. It was hard, punishing work, and once the dinghy slipped round and they lost ten yards before they could straighten up again. They kept some way away from the coaster, going parallel to the side. Collins knew the tide would be much stronger streaming round the jetty and they would have to work up almost abreast of the fo'c's'le-head before they dared fall alongside. Just beside the ladder that went up from the deck on to the stern there was a lead-hole, used for a spring line, and he aimed to come in alongside that.

Their arms were moving slower and slower now, both hands in the water almost up to the elbows, pulling back on the paddles, feeling as if they were scooping liquid mud, sliding the paddles forward again under the surface, fighting the tide inch by inch, mouths open, gasping desperately, aching all through their bodies. At last they were abreast of the fo'c's'le-head, and with a quick slant, stroking the paddles frantically, they fell in against the side of the coaster.

Quickly Collins dropped his paddle and stood up, the frail dinghy almost overturning, and as the tide swept them back to the stern, Mickey using all his force to keep them close into the side, Collins reached out and with a final stretching lunge hooked his fingers into the lead-hole.

Mickey took the line, and making one end fast to a ring in the bows of the dinghy, stood up and tried to reach through the lead-hole and get a turn on one of the bitts on the deck inside. The dinghy dipped and swayed precariously under their feet. Mickey tried again, holding a bight of the line in one hand, trying to loop it over the bitt. He failed.

Suddenly the murmuring sound of the Guards' voices stopped and Collins heard the stamp of boots on the iron deck. He held Mickey's wrist close to his face so he could see the time by the wrist watch.

10.02 P.M.

Collins waited until he heard the clank of the bucket in one of the Guards' hands, then the dull thudding of feet on the gangway.

He moved in the dinghy so Mickey could get a firm grip in the lead-hole. Then, with his left hand still in the lead-hole, he made a small spring, hanging from the side first by his right hand and, with a quick twist, bringing his left hand up beside it. He hung like that, his fingers resting on the flat surface of the top of the bulwark, listening to the feet going away along the jetty towards the town. This side of the coaster was quite dark, but, dangling there, looking up at his fingers, which seemed to be white, bloated sausages, he waited for the Guards to get well clear of the other side before he pulled himself up. Every second he expected the crushing blow of a rifle-butt on his fingers.

When he was sure the Guards walking along the jetty would be out of view behind the structure of the wheel-house, Collins pulled himself up slowly until his eyes were level with the top of the bulwark and he could see over the side and across the deck.

It was as he had hoped. The Guard left on the coaster was leaning over the far side, his back towards Collins, watching his mates going up to the town. Any moment

132

now, Collins thought, he'll turn round to make the tour of the deck as he did last night.

With another pull-and-swing Collins got his left foot hooked over the side, then the final rolling heave, face down on the bulwark, body flattened out, and he went across the top and his bare feet touched the deck silently on the other side. His knees bent quickly and then he was hidden behind the side of the hatch, huddled against the coaming.

He crouched there, listening. When he heard no sound from the Guard, he lay flat on his belly across the narrow passage that separated the side of the raised hatch from the bulwark, and, reaching his hand through the lead-hole, took a line from Mickey and made it fast to the bitt. When he had done that, he crouched again behind the hatch and, moving along to the dark corner against the after-bulkhead, underneath the ladder that came down from the stern on to the deck he was now on, he raised his head slowly above the level of the hatch.

The Guard was still leaning over the side, looking now towards their ship. Not bothering to hide now, knowing they must hurry, Collins leaned over the side and, stretching his arms down, caught Mickey's waiting arms above the wrists. Mickey was too short to be able to reach the side on his own. Now, with a spring and Collins lifting, his head and shoulders came over the bulwark, and then he too was crouching behind the hatch.

The tarpaulin covering the hatch overlapped the sides, hanging down for about two feet. Sliding their hands underneath, keeping their heads just over the top so that they could watch the Guard, Collins and Mickey fumbled for the handles of the nearest hatch cover. Collins found this, looked at Mickey. Mickey nodded. Still watching the Guard, they lifted off the first cover and laid it gently on the deck at their feet.

They took off the next one, then Mickey, standing upright, his face white and taut as he looked over at the Guard's back no more than ten yards away, swung his legs under the tarpaulin as if he were climbing into bed and lowered himself into the hold. Collins went down on his knees and put his head under the tarpaulin just in time to see Mickey wriggling across the top layer of sugar

133

sacks. There was a space of about two feet between the sugar sacks and the hatch covers.

Crouched in the corner under the ladder again, the shadows of the hatch, the after-bulkhead, and the ladder overhead protecting him if the Guard were to turn round suddenly, Collins waited for Mickey to locate the boxes. Now that he was no longer doing anything, Collins felt nervousness clutch at his stomach again. His eyes smarted, and he realized suddenly that he had been watching the Guard so hard he had forgotten to blink. Nor had he noticed the increased strength of the breeze coming in from the sea. The sky was still dark; waiting there in the corner, he was glad for that at least.

When the Guard did turn round from leaning over the side, Collins was almost unprepared. He hunched down so fast that he felt his neck crick. He waited for the sound of footsteps, but when after a while he didn't hear them, he lifted his head again and saw the Guard sitting on the hatch with his back towards him. In a sudden flood of hope, he thought: We're going to do it. It's going to be all right. He's not going to walk round the deck tonight, I won't have to use the pipe.

There was no sound from the hold. Squatting in his corner, wondering how Mickey was getting on, Collins felt one of his legs start to ache, and he shifted his bare feet on the deck to ease the slight cramp. The top of the hatch was some three feet from the deck, and he was kneeling on one knee, with the other leg braced under him. This was the only position in which he could see across the hatches and yet be able to duck quickly if the Guard looked round. It was an uncomfortable position to hold. His knee and the muscles in the other leg fluttered.

For Chrissakes, how long is he going to be down there? Collins thought. It must be getting late. He calculated that they had been aboard a good ten minutes. That left another twenty before the Guards came back with the supper.

If they took as long as they had last night.

He listened anxiously, straining to hear the hollow thumps on the jetty that would announce the return of the Guards. The wind felt damp against his face, and the mist clouded past the light over the gangway.

What the hell's that crazy clown doing under there, anyway? Collins raged. He must be counting it dollar by dollar.

Come on. *Come on!*

At first Collins wasn't sure he had really heard anything. He was so keyed up that he thought it might be an involuntary sound he had made himself. Then it came again. A small rasping noise . . . and then the tarpaulin dented outwards and he knew it was Mickey.

Collins moved the tarpaulin back gently. Mickey's face was pouring sweat, and his short hair was plastered flat. His mouth hung wide open, and he stared up at Collins with a loose, idiotic expression.

He nodded limply.

Keeping his eyes on the Guard's back all the time, Collins lowered himself into the hold.

# 14

EASING THE TARPAULIN back into place over his head, Collins lay down on the hard roughness of the sugar sacks. Beside him Mickey sprawled with his cheek resting against a sack; his breath came in rasping jerks, the only sound in the stagnant, putrid-sweet blackness of the hold.

Collins crawled forward, put his mouth close to Mickey's ear.

"You O.K.?" he whispered.

Mickey's head stirred, and they wriggled forward together across the tops of the sugar sacks. Once Collins started a hatch cover out of place with his back, but he remembered to "freeze" before letting it down gently into place. The atmosphere was overpowering. The sacks had been loaded some days before, and the sun on the iron deck and sides had baked out the sickly-sweet smell till it was as strong as fermenting wine. Loose grains clung to their sweat-soaked shirts and faces, scratching the skin.

They were near the centre of the hold now, and for

135

some reason the bags were slightly higher here than at the side. Collins's body was pressed hard down on the sacks, and he felt his back graze the covers overhead. The rough sacking rubbed his cheek.

Finally they passed this point and were on the far side of the hold. Suddenly Collins's outstretched hand touched the hard bulk of a displaced sack. He twisted his head forward. Mickey motioned him to stay there, then crawled ahead. Moving over to the right where Mickey had been, Collins found himself on the edge of a cavity, and, reaching down with one hand, he touched the flat wood surfaces of the boxes.

No wonder he was so long, Collins thought. He counted two layers of sacks above the boxes, which were about five feet long. Six sacks. Mickey must have had to shift at least six to get to the boxes.

He couldn't see Mickey's face across the gap, but when he heard him hiss he knew he must be ready, and, leaning far over, he felt with his fingers for the edges of the nearest box. Lying there, scraping his fingers on the even edges of the box, trying to get a grip, he thought in sudden panic that they were pulling at different boxes. He tried working his fingers down between the back of the box and the sacks. There must be a handle somewhere.

Suddenly he felt the box tilt up from the far end, and, putting his hands underneath, he was able to prize out his end. He pulled it up on to the sacks, then waited for Mickey to go down into the cavity to lift up the other end so that they could drag the box clear.

Collins was very tired now. It was only about seven yards from here to the side, but his lungs felt as though they would burst, and his head ached and spun from the swamping smell of the hold. He lay on his back, reaching his arms over and behind his head, moving the box foot by foot. It was made of wood, but was bound and ribbed with metal, and several times a sharp edge caught in the sacks and Collins had to push it back a little, then lift it past the place where the box had caught.

After what seemed a timeless dream Collins felt his feet strike the side and, looking up, saw the black underside of the tarpaulin above him. His first thought was to find out what the time was, and only then did he realize that for the last few yards he hadn't felt Mickey's guiding hands at the far end of the box.

Collins let go the box and, turning over on his belly, peered across the sacks, trying to see where Mickey was He groaned involuntarily, wiping the sweat from his eyes. He shook his head, trying to clear the buzzing hum in his ears. Then he crawled back into the fetid atmosphere of the hold.

Mickey was lying with his head between his outstretched arms in a dead faint. Collins's groping hand touched the wet, matted hair on Mickey's head before he could even see him. He reached forward, trying to get his arms under Mickey's armpits. All the time Collins felt himself moving slower and slower, the ringing in his ears stronger now, hardly able to keep his eyes open, thinking all the time: We could have done it, we could have been away by now. Locking his fingers together behind Mickey's back, Collins started inching the limp body back towards the side.

He had got about half-way when the squall broke over the ship, beating down on the stiff tarpaulin over the hatch covers with a noise like gunshot pellets drumming on a hollow tub. Dragging Mickey the last two yards in one back-wrenching, arm-jellying effort, Collins propped him up against the side. Not caring any longer about the Guard, his mind befuddled by the odour of the overheated sugar sacks, Collins scrounched back the tarpaulin, letting the driving rain fall on his and Mickey's upturned faces.

With a roll of his head and a choking groan Mickey came to. His wide-open eyes focussed blurrily on Collins's face. The warm rain drenched into the hold and washed away their sweat and exhaustion like a shower.

When Mickey had recovered, Collins looked at the time.

10.25 P.M.

Ten minutes at the outside, he thought. But maybe this squall will keep the other two in town. If they haven't already left. He listened, trying to shut out the rain noise, waiting to hear running feet on the jetty.

"The other one," Mickey whispered feebly. "Where's the other one?"

137

Collins jerked his thumb towards the stern. He must be sheltering somewhere back there, he thought. I must have been crazy to whip that tarpaulin back like that. He's standing well back on the stern, otherwise he would have been bound to see us. He slipped the iron pipe from his pocket, turning it over in his hand, hesitating. No, Collins thought. It'll have to be this way now. Once this squall blows over, they'll be back from town. As it is now, it would cover us.

Collins slipped the two rag rings off the end of the pipe. Mickey looked at him questioningly. Collins shrugged, then, taking a quick look round first, lifted himself out of the hold and crouched on the deck.

His bare feet made no sound going up the ladder on to the stern. Keeping close to the superstructure of the wheelhouse, he went round the curve of the stern in a fast, noiseless glide.

The Guard was standing on the other side of the stern, about ten feet from the ladder. He was looking along the deck out to sea, watching the dark line of the squall cloud. Collins could smell the harsh odour of black tobacco.

The Guard was standing obliquely against the rail. Coming round the curve of the superstructure, Collins suddenly saw the flat profile under the three-cornered hat. The Guard's rifle was slung across his back.

With the palm of his left hand, his left cheek, and his back flat against the superstructure, Collins calculated the distance between him and the Guard. He didn't dare turn back. The slightest movement and the Guard might see him out of the corner of his eye.

Now—do it now. Collins longed to turn his head to look up the jetty. If the Guards were coming back, they would see him easily. It was dark, but not that dark. Now, he thought, quick, now. Yellow Shirt. Remember *that*.

Collins shifted his right foot out to the side, tensed himself, bent forward, and gripped the iron pipe firm in his hand. It slipped in his wet palm and hit the deck with a clang.

The Guard spun round with a funny high shriek of surprise. Frantically groping for the pipe, Collins saw

138

the Guard tugging at his waist. At the instant that his fingers at last closed round the pipe Collins lunged at the Guard, sticking out his left hand to ward off what he thought would be a revolver. Towering over the small, stooped Indian, he swung the pipe down hard on the side of the Guard's head, crashing through the projecting corner of the hat, falling forward on top of the Guard with the force of the blow.

A white-hot searing pain flashed up his left forearm.

The Guard crumpled towards the deck, and Collins slammed the pipe down again on the now unprotected head, believing that the first blow had been deflected by the hat.

For a moment he stood over the Guard, panting, the pipe ready in his hand, looking down at the rolled-back whites of the Guard's eyes. He noticed then the short bayonet lying beyond the head and was surprised. He had somehow assumed it was a bullet that had grazed his arm.

Without stopping to look at the damage to his arm, he picked the Guard up under his armpits and dragged him round the stern towards the ladder on the far side. The rain was still streaming down, and there was nobody on the jetty yet. At every step round the stern he expected to see the two fingers coming down the incline from the town. The muzzle of the Guard's rifle kept catching him across the legs, and he stopped and unslung it off the Guard and tossed it over the side into the bay.

At the top of the ladder he turned and saw Mickey standing below on the deck. The water was rilling down his white, drawn face.

"What happened?" Mickey said hoarsely. "When I heard him yell out— It's ten thirty."

"I dropped the goddam pipe. He stuck me with a shiv. For Chrissakes, let's shove him in the hold and get outta here quick."

They got the Guard down the ladder and laid him in the hold, took out the box, and pulled the tarpaulin back into place. Mickey went over the side first. Collins picked up the long, metal-ribbed, dull-green box, hardly noticing the sudden warm throb in his hurt arm, and lowered one end to Mickey. Mickey laid the box lengthways in the dinghy, then, gripping the lead-hole, straddling the box with his feet, held the dinghy against the side while Collins let go the line off the bitt. It was nearly high water now, and it took very little effort to hold the dinghy firm. Collins let himself down over the side, taking one last look at the jetty. Hanging by his arms, he set his feet down carefully on either side of the box.

The ends of the box overlapped the bows and stern of the dinghy by a few inches. The dinghy was meant for only one person, and now, with the added weight of the box, there were scarcely two inches of freeboard. Sitting astride the box, bending far forward, Collins and Mickey started paddling towards the end of the jetty.

As they rounded the coaster, there was still enough tide to keep pushing them back, and they almost got jammed athwart the bows. Collins dropped his paddle and pushing the dinghy away with both hands, while Mickey paddled furiously to keep her head against the tide. At last they were alongside the jetty, and here it was even worse. There was no room for the inshore paddler, and they didn't have time to take the dinghy out into the bay where the tide would be slacker.

"We'll have to pull her round," Mickey panted.

They stopped trying to paddle, and, grasping the slimy timber strut that went alongside the jetty, began to pull the dinghy towards the far end. The edges of the box cut the insides of their thighs, and their hands slipped on the green filth that corroded the strut. The rain was still coming down, slanting into their faces, so that when they raised their heads they were instantly blinded. Inch by inch, groping and tugging, they found their way along to the end of the jetty. Again and again Collins wanted to stop, to hang his arms round the strut, rest his face against the soft mushy growth to let the heaviness drain from his arms and back.

But, never sure whether the hollow ringing was the footsteps on the jetty of the returning Guards or only in his head, he would reach forward and dig his fingers into the slipperiness, beginning to feel the soreness in his hurt arm now, and drag the dinghy along another foot or so. When they had started working along the strut they had been in unison—reaching forward together—pulling along to their hands—reaching forward together—but now they were dragging the dinghy along just anyhow. They didn't talk, they had no breath for that.

They still had several yards to go when, as suddenly as it had started, the rain stopped and the outer edge of the squall passed inland. Now that the hissing, splashing noise of the rain was gone, they were more than ever conscious of their own gasping struggle, knowing that they were already late, that the Guards would be back any minute now that the squall had passed.

At the end of the jetty, as they turned the dinghy round the supporting timber foot, a small bobbing ripple broke over the side of the dinghy. Looking down, Collins saw that there was less than an inch of freeboard. The rain had covered the bottom boards. Another ripple like the last would capsize them. He let go of the jetty and, using his hands, tried to bail the water out.

Mickey stopped pulling and looked round.

"Go on, go on," Collins sobbed.

Slower and slower the dinghy crept along the front of the jetty. At last they had reached the far supporting timber, and Collins stopped bailing and helped Mickey turn the dinghy down the other side.

The dark stern of their ship loomed high above them. Collins looked frantically for the ladder. He knew it must be well past 10.30 by now. He tried to whistle, but he couldn't control his breath. The remaining tide was strong enough to carry them under the stern, and as they clung to the strut on this side, looking up at the stern-rail, there came a long slithering clatter and they saw the ladder snaking down from the fantail. With one last push they got out from the jetty, and, beating and ploughing at the water with their paddles, they made for the ladder, which hung to the water now, just on the other side of the stern.

Seven feet away . . . six . . . four.

Mickey reached forward in the bows to grab the ladder.

Collins could hear Svensson calling down to them to hurry. He sounded very far away.

A tremor somewhere beneath them, something stirring, the sudden raucous groan of the ship's siren, and instantly a white churning foam enveloped the dinghy, creaming over the sides, completely swamping them.

Mickey yelled, twisting on to his back as he fell forward, his hands striving for the ladder.

Tipped backward by the erupting water thrown up by the propeller, Collins had time to see the box slide sideways into the foam like a coffin. Then his head was under, his ears filled with a hollow roar. When he came to the surface again, the propeller had stopped—the regulation engine-room test was over—and the bubbles were bouncing on the dark water as it slowly overlapped the white of the foam. Mickey was hanging on the ladder, his arms jammed round the slats, one foot on the lower rung.

*"Where did it go, where d'it go?"* Collins shouted.

Water filled his mouth, and, summoning up all that was left of his strength, the sudden immersion clearing his head in an agonizing purge of realization that it had all been for nothing, that the box was gone, Collins ducked and pulled himself under in a long dive.

He came up again directly under the ladder, his lungs feeling like clenched fists, and Mickey leaned down and caught his arm. They clung together, a dripping, indistinct mass at the foot of the ladder. Collins struggled to free himself, then suddenly collapsed, finally exhausted. Something went out of him then as if he had died. Slowly climbing the ladder behind Mickey, he finally fell over the stern-rail at Svensson's feet.

Svensson helped them both down the companionway to the cabin. From the deck came the sound of the crew as they took in the gangway. Mickey flung himself on to the bunk. Collins slumped over on the bench under the porthole. Svensson left them there, went out and shut the door. On deck the crew were letting-go the lines, and the winches were thumping in the night.

Collins got up after a while and looked out of the porthole. But the ship was loaded now; the porthole was below the jetty and he couldn't see the coaster. It didn't matter any more, though.

Mickey came over and touched his arm. He looked down and saw that the hand was full of blood coming from his forearm.

"That looks bad, Big Jay," Mickey said, rolling back

142

the sleeve. There was a deep four-inch gash. The flesh at the edges was white from the salt water.

"You'd better get the Old Man to look at that once we're at sea," Mickey said.

Three blasts on the siren, and the ship was going astern, the jetty slipping past the porthole.

"You can tell him you cut it with your own knife. Slipped in your hand when you were cutting something. Tell him anything—it doesn't matter now," Mickey said.

As the ship turned to go out into the channel, Collins, still looking out of the porthole, saw the two Guards walking along the jetty towards the coaster. They must have stopped for a drink when the squall came.

The door opened and Svensson came in.

"It's all right. Nobody say anything. They don't notice you're not there at the let-go." He saw Collins's arm and drew his breath in sharply.

"Boy, that's bad," he said. He looked at Collins quickly. "You have trouble?"

"No. It was easy." Collins stared out of the porthole, watching the wake of the ship. They were already too far away to see the Guards on the coaster clearly any more.

"You have to get that seen to, Big Jay," Svensson said.

"In a minute."

"It's goin' to be pretty stiff tomorrow," Mickey said. "It'll still be sore when we get up north."

"That's all right." Collins watched the dark receding line of the jetty.

"You got some place you can rest up when you get ashore?" Mickey asked. "You won't be able to do much with that arm for a couple of weeks."

"I got a place I can go, all right," Collins said.

(Please turn page)

you'll also want to read

## THE MAN WITH TWO SHADOWS
### by Robin Maugham

When Peter Grant returned to the Middle East to work for British Intelligence, he thought he had recovered from the wartime injury that caused him to black out—to forget who he was and what he did . . . but he was wrong, and he suddenly found himself caught in a net of love, intrigue and murder. "Fascinating study in depth of a man in creepy conflict with a part of his own mind."—New York Times. (35¢)

## SHOULDER THE SKY
### by George Leonard

A powerful novel of young fliers in World War II, who are stationed at a Georgia Air Force base and waiting to get into combat, when crisis comes into their lives. Crisis—in the form of a beautiful woman, a tragic night-flying mission, and a court martial. "Engrossing novel . . . a shattering climax."—Jackson, Tennessee Sun. (50¢)

---

These books available at your local newsstand, or send price indicated plus 10¢ per copy for mailing costs to Berkley Publishing Corp., 101 Fifth Avenue, New York 3, New York.